"Maybe I should invite myself to dinner," Matt said lightly.

Olivia looked at him. "Seriously?"

"Seriously." He grinned. "Single guys don't get many home-cooked meals."

Once again, she hesitated before answering, "Well, I know Thea will be thrilled if you stay to dinner."

"Only Thea? What about you?"

"Are you digging for a compliment?"

"Everyone likes compliments."

"Okay. I'm glad you want to have dinner with us. There. Are you satisfied?"

Now that the tone of their conversation had changed, he decided to make one more attempt to burrow through her defenses. "I was hoping you'd say you liked me, too."

"Of course I like you, Matt. You're part of the family."

Because they were now approaching her mother's house, he let the comment go without answering.

THE CRANDALL LAKE CHRONICLES:
Small town, big hearts

Dear Readers,

I love small-town life. I'm a small-town girl myself, so I understand what it's like to be surrounded by people who know you and care about you. I've put a lot of myself and my upbringing into this series, which is one of the main reasons it's been such a joy to write. I'm sure my parents are smiling down from heaven when they see how much their love and guidance has influenced my life.

I've also gotten very attached to the characters in these books—characters always become real to authors—and have loved exploring their lives and loves. I hope you enjoy reading Olivia's story as much as I enjoyed writing it.

Come visit me on Facebook at Facebook.com/patricia.kay.56 and chat with me on Twitter: @PatriciaAKay. I love to hear from readers!

Warmly,

Patricia Kay

The Man She Should Have Married

Patricia Kay

HARLEQUIN® SPECIAL EDITION®

Recycling programs
for this product may
not exist in your area.

ISBN-13: 978-0-373-65989-0

The Man She Should Have Married

Copyright © 2016 by Patricia A. Kay

Printed in U.S.A.

Having formerly written as Trisha Alexander,
Patricia Kay is a *USA TODAY* bestselling author
of more than forty-eight novels of contemporary
romance and women's fiction. She lives in Houston,
Texas. To learn more about her, visit her website at
patriciakay.com.

This book is dedicated to all the amazing women in my life. I don't know how any woman survives without girlfriends. Your friendship and support has meant the world to me. I love you all!

Chapter One

Crandall Lake, Texas
Mid-October...

Olivia Britton grinned at her cousin, the newly married Eve Crenshaw. "I'm so happy you're here!"

Eve laughed. "You've already said that at least ten times."

"I know. But I *am*. I've missed you." In fact, Olivia couldn't believe how much she'd missed Eve.

"Oh, come on, Liv. I've only been gone six weeks. And we've texted and talked on the phone almost every day."

"It's not the same," Olivia insisted. "You're not here. We can't meet for lunch or have dinner together or just sit and talk for hours. And Thea misses you, too!" Thea, short for Dorothea, was Olivia's four-year-old daughter.

Eve nodded. "I know. But no matter where I am, I'll always be here for you...*and* Thea. You know that." She drank some of her wine, then reached over and squeezed Olivia's knee. "And I'm here now."

The cousins were sitting on either end of the sofa in Olivia's living room. Their children were settled upstairs for the night and it was blessedly quiet, so Olivia hoped they were all asleep. They should be. It was after eleven, and she and Eve could finally talk without curious ears.

Olivia sighed. Eve wasn't just her cousin. She was also her best friend, someone Olivia had always looked up to, someone she'd known was just minutes away for a hug, a shoulder to cry on or a listening ear. The only person in the world who knew everything about her—well, *almost* everything—and could be completely trusted.

But now Eve would be spending the majority of her time in either Los Angeles or Nashville, where her new husband (and the twins' birth father), the famous and fabulous Adam Crenshaw—composer and lead singer of the band Version II—had two magnificent homes.

Eve, along with her twins Nathan and Natalie, had come back to Crandall Lake for the weekend to join in the family celebration of Olivia's mother's birthday.

Olivia sighed again. She was thrilled for Eve. Her cousin had waited a long time for some true happiness. But Olivia also loved seeing her daughter with her older cousins, both of whom Thea adored. And now that Eve and the twins had settled in Los Angeles for the school year, nothing would ever be the same again, no matter what Eve said.

Eve was still talking, still making an obvious attempt to reassure Olivia. "I'll be coming to Crandall Lake a lot. And you'll be visiting us wherever we are. And you know, I've been thinking. If you want to, you and Thea can even travel with us when Adam has a concert and we're able to go with him."

"I have a job, you know." But wouldn't it be wonderful to be free of everything tying her down and just take Thea and go, the way Eve was suggesting? "Besides, I don't think I should leave my mom." Norma was newly diagnosed as a diabetic—something their family seemed to be genetically disposed to—and was having some trouble dealing with the disease.

Eve gave Olivia a sideways look. "Stella's here." Stella was Olivia's younger sister and she lived within walking distance of their family home. "You said yourself she's really stepped up to the plate and has educated herself about the disease so that she can help your mom."

"I know, but…" Olivia evaded Eve's gaze.

"Let's talk about the *real* reason. You're afraid Vivienne would make trouble for you if you moved."

Olivia made a face. Her mother-in-law hated her in direct proportion to the possessiveness she felt for Thea, her only grandchild, the daughter of her perfect younger son, who had died so tragically in the crash of his Black Hawk helicopter in Afghanistan.

"Am I right? Or am I right?" Eve pressed.

"You're right."

"She's a piece of work, isn't she?"

"That's a kind way of putting it."

"I'll never understand her." Eve finished her wine and set the glass on the coffee table in front of them.

"I'm not sure anyone does." Olivia got up and retrieved the still-half-full bottle of Merlot she'd opened earlier. She poured more into Eve's glass. "Even Matt says she's just used to getting her own way, and when she doesn't, look out."

She was referring to Matt Britton, her brother-in-law, Vivienne's oldest son. He'd always been good to Olivia, in spite of his mother. In fact, since Mark's death, Olivia wasn't sure how she'd have coped with her mother-in-law if not for Matt.

From day one, Vivienne Britton had been furious that Mark, her obvious favorite child, had wanted to marry "a nobody" like Olivia Dubrovnik instead of Charlotte Chambers, the daughter of the Brittons' oldest friends. Charlotte was "our kind" and "perfect for you" as she'd told Mark many times, once even in Olivia's hearing. It still amazed Olivia that Mark had defied his mother, because in all other things he had always done what she wanted him to do.

"Let's not talk about her anymore." Olivia poured more wine into her own glass and sat down again, curling her bare legs under her.

Eve smiled. "Good idea. Instead, let's talk about you dating again."

"I'm only *thinking* about dating again," Olivia corrected. "I haven't really decided. Besides, it's not like there's a line of eligible men out the door."

There *was* one person who interested her, and for a moment, she was tempted to tell Eve about him, but pushed the urge away, because the situation was impossible. She felt a bit guilty about *not* telling Eve, because normally she told her everything, but in this case, her gut told her it was best not to put her feelings into words.

"The reason guys aren't lining up is because no one knows you're ready," Eve said.

"I can hardly make an announcement."

"No, but I can get the word out."

Olivia stared at her. "What are you going to do? Put

a notice in the *Courier*?" Eve had worked for the *Cran-dall Lake Courier* before marrying Adam in August.

Eve grinned, a sly look in her eyes. "No, but I just might mention it casually to Austin when we see him Sunday morning."

"Austin!" Olivia was startled. Austin Crenshaw was one of Adam's younger brothers. A successful lawyer, he took care of all Adam's personal and professional legal and financial matters. "Why would *he* care?"

"Surely you saw how he was checking you out at the wedding," Eve said. Austin had been Adam's best man, and Olivia had served as Eve's matron of honor.

"That's ridiculous!" Olivia said. "He was just being polite to his new sister-in-law's cousin."

Eve shook her head knowingly. "Nope. He's interested. I know the signs. And he'd be perfect for you."

"That's crazy. I am *so* not in his league."

"Why are you constantly putting yourself down? He couldn't *find* anyone better if he tried!"

Olivia loved that her cousin was always so loyal, but she had to face facts. "C'mon, Eve. If he'd really been interested, as you say, why hasn't he called me or something?"

"I don't know. But I'm going to find out."

"No, no. Please don't say anything to him."

"I'll just casually bring up your name Sunday."

"No! Please, Eve. I really don't want you to."

"It's not a big deal," Eve insisted. "Austin and I have a great relationship. Since Adam and I got married, I've really gotten to know him. We've sort of bonded. And he's a really great guy."

Olivia knew, just from the determined look on Eve's face, that she was not going to be dissuaded. It was useless to keep trying. Because, if she did, Eve would eventually wonder why. "Okay, but don't say anything in front of the kids." Eve and her twins were meeting Austin for breakfast Sunday.

"Don't worry." Eve smiled, happy now she'd gotten her way. "I'll be discreet. The kids won't hear me."

"Thing is, I don't want him to think I put you up to talking to him." The very idea made Olivia cringe. Why had she even mentioned she was thinking about dating? She should have known Eve would latch on to that and start suggesting possible candidates. She gave a mental sigh. Austin *did* seem nice. Plus he certainly was easy on the eyes. All the Crenshaw men were. And since the one man who *did* interest her was completely and totally off-limits…

"Quit worrying," Eve said. "That's my job, remember?"

Olivia smiled. Worrying *was* Eve's job, always had been. She was the conservative one, the cautious one. Olivia had always been more impulsive, more willing to take a chance.

But that was before she'd had Thea.

Before she was a mother.

Now her first priority would always be her daughter, and that meant she had to think carefully before she did anything that might negatively impact Thea's life in any way.

"Seriously, Eve," she said, "I'm not in any hurry. If I do get into another relationship, he'd have to be pretty special…after Mark." It made her sad to think about Mark, who was her first love. They'd only been married months before he went to Afghanistan. They'd had so little time. His life had been cut so short, and he'd died so young. And without ever holding or knowing his daughter, except for photos and images on Skype.

"I know," Eve said. "You have plenty of time, and I'm

sure, once the guys around here—Austin included—know you're ready, there'll be no shortage of possible candidates."

Olivia rolled her eyes. She wasn't anywhere near as confident as Eve that men would be lining up to take on a widow with a small child.

The cousins continued to talk for another hour or so, but when the Wedgewood clock on the mantel chimed one o'clock, Eve yawned and stretched. "I'm beat."

"Me, too. We'd better get to bed. Tomorrow's a big day." Olivia got up and took Eve's glass. "You can use the bathroom first. I'll take these out to the kitchen and be there in a minute." The cousins were sharing Olivia's bedroom and the king-size bed she and Mark had so happily purchased together.

As she rinsed out the wineglasses and put them in the dishwasher, Olivia decided she was going to make the most of the weekend. She wasn't going to think about her mother-in-law or about Eve going back to LA or the way Olivia's own life had not turned out the way she'd once imagined it would.

She was just going to relax, have fun, eat some salty and sugary junk food, and thoroughly enjoy having Eve and the kids home again.

No matter what.

"It's a gorgeous day, isn't it?" Eve exclaimed. "I love autumn in the Hill Country."

"Me, too," Olivia said, linking her arm through Eve's.

The cousins were strolling through the grounds where Crandall Lake's Fall Festival, an annual celebration featuring music, food, games and rides as well as various craft items for sale, took place every October.

Norma Dubrovnik, Olivia's mother, and her older

sister, Anna Cermak, Eve's mother, were walking up ahead. Between the older women and the two younger women were Nathan and Natalie, with Olivia's Thea between them. Each twin had one of Thea's hands, and every few steps they'd lift their little cousin and swing her out, then set her back on her feet again. Thea's delighted giggles peppered the air.

"Liv, Eve, hurry up! You're so poky!" Olivia looked around to see her younger sister Stella waving and calling to them.

"We're coming," Eve said as they caught up to where Stella stood.

"I thought you'd gone home or something," Olivia said. "You disappeared."

"I spied my boss by the pizza booth, and I went over to talk to her," Stella said. She was laughing, her fresh face and bright eyes a clear sign that life hadn't yet dealt her any devastating blows. Olivia hoped it never would.

Just as Eve and Olivia reached the rest of their group, who were now gathered by the crowded booth where hot funnel cakes were cooked and sold, Olivia's mother said, "It's so hot." She was mopping at her forehead with a tissue.

Olivia frowned. It wasn't hot. In fact, the weather was perfect. Sixty-eight degrees and sunny, according to her phone just thirty minutes earlier.

"I don't feel good," her mother continued. Her face had drained of color, and she swayed.

"Norma," Eve's mother said, reaching out to put her arm around her sister. "C'mon, let's go sit on that bench over there." She met Olivia's eyes. "She's shaking."

Alarmed, Olivia said, "Mom. What's wr—" But she never had a chance to finish what she was going to say because at that moment Norma just seemed to fold in on herself and slumped to the ground. "Mom!" Olivia dropped down to where her mother lay.

"Norma!" This came from Eve's mother, who knelt next to Olivia.

People around them buzzed with concern and several onlookers crouched down.

"Mom," Stella said, patting Norma, who was struggling to sit up. "What happened?"

"I—I don't know. I just feel so weak."

"Did you eat breakfast this morning?" Olivia asked.

"What's going on here?" said an authoritative male voice.

Olivia looked up. She knew that voice. It was Dr. Groves, Thea's pediatrician. "Dr. Groves, this is my mother. She said she was hot and she was sweating, but her face was white. Then she just collapsed. I think it's a low blood sugar reaction. She's a diabetic. Newly diagnosed."

"On oral meds or insulin?"

"Oral," Stella said. "She takes them in the morning and again at night."

"When did she eat last?"

"I—I had some toast for breakfast," Norma said weakly.

"Nothing since? No protein?" Dr. Groves asked.

Stella shook her head. "I don't think so. We've been here since ten o'clock."

Olivia mentally sighed. Her mother still didn't seem to realize the importance of eating at regular intervals and keeping her meals balanced, even though they'd already had several discussions about the potential consequences.

"She needs sugar, fast," Dr. Groves said. "She's having a low blood sugar reaction. This happens when diabetics are on meds and don't eat the right things often enough."

"She can have my funnel cake," one of the onlookers said. The woman, someone Olivia didn't know, thrust forward her paper plate containing a sugared funnel cake. "I just got it."

"That's good," the doctor said, "but some orange juice would be faster acting. Once we get her blood sugar stabilized, she'll need something more substantial, with protein, like a hot dog or one of those chicken drumsticks they're selling."

"I'll go get some orange juice," Nathan piped up. "There's a juice stand right over there." He pointed to one about a hundred feet away. "I have tickets!" He held up a strip of the tickets used in lieu of money at all the booths.

In all the confusion Olivia had lost track of Thea, and she looked around as Nathan ran off, and Dr. Groves continued to monitor her mother, but she didn't see Thea. She saw Natalie, though, and called to her. "Where's Thea, honey?"

Natalie frowned and looked around. "She…she was just here."

Olivia's mother was now sitting on a nearby bench, with her sister, the doctor and Stella in attendance. They were feeding her some funnel cake. Olivia, who wasn't yet alarmed, figured Thea was simply hidden by one of the members of the group of people waiting on funnel cakes or lured by the earlier commotion of her mother's collapse. She headed toward Eve, who still stood near the booth with Natalie. At the moment, the young girl seemed a lot older than her almost-twelve years, with her worried face and frightened eyes. She took her responsibility of watching after Thea very seriously.

"Thea!" Olivia called as she walked through the clusters of people. "Thea, honey, where are you?"

Eve frowned and hurried toward Olivia. "What's wrong?"

"I don't see Thea anywhere." Now Olivia's voice held an edge of fear.

"Natalie?" Eve said, eyeing her daughter.

Natalie looked stricken. "Mom, I—I don't know where she is."

"But you were holding her hand, honey. You and Nathan said you were going to watch her today."

"I know, Mom, but Auntie Norma fainted and…and I must have let go of her hand. I—I don't know where Thea went." The last word was a wail, and Natalie's eyes filled with tears. "I'm sorry."

"Oh, my God," Olivia said. Her heart had begun to hammer, and full-blown panic had set in. Now she looked around frantically. "Thea! Thea! Where *are* you?"

By now, several people had stopped whatever they were doing and were staring at her. One of them said to Eve, "What's wrong?"

Eve quickly explained. "She's probably just wandered off, but–"

"But what if she hasn't?" Olivia cried. "What if…" She couldn't even finish the thought. Horrible images flashed through her mind in the space of seconds. Thea was so little. So sweet and innocent and trusting. And so very beautiful with her blond curly hair, the exact shade of her father's, and her shining brown eyes, just like Olivia's own. Olivia closed her eyes, also thinking how inquisitive her daughter was, how *interested* in things, the way she would talk to strangers. "Please, God," she whispered. "Please, God, let her be okay."

Her greatest fear was losing Thea. Losing Mark had been hard enough, but losing Thea was unthinkable.

"Liv, she's okay, I know she is," Eve said. "Let's look methodically. Think, Natalie, did she say anything?"

Natalie's tear-stained face screwed up in thought. "I—I think she said something about a kitty right before Auntie Norma said she didn't feel good."

"A kitten!" Olivia said. "Maybe…maybe she saw a kitten." She looked at Eve. "You know how she loves cats. She…she's been begging for one for months." Olivia had been waiting, thinking she'd surprise Thea at Christmas.

"Let's get some of these people looking. She can't have gone far," Eve said. She turned to one of the nearby groups. "Her little girl's wandered off. We need help looking for her."

"I'll notify security," a man said, taking out his cell phone. "I know the man in charge. What's the little girl's name?"

Within moments, Eve had organized a search party armed with Thea's description and information, the head of security had arrived and been briefed, and 9-1-1 had also been called.

Olivia felt sick with fear. It was all she could do not to break down completely, but she knew if she did, she'd be useless. She forced herself to take deep breaths… and *think*. Thank God for Eve. And thank God, Olivia's mother didn't know what was happening, because Thea was *her* only grandchild, too, and totally adored.

But it wouldn't be long before Norma would find out about Thea, because Olivia could see two police officers coming toward them, and the head of security here at the festival had just told her they were going to get an announcement on the loudspeaker so that everyone attending the festival would be on the lookout for Thea.

"Olivia?" The oldest police officer, a man Olivia recognized as Tom Nicholls, looked at her. His wife, Betty, was a nurse at the Crandall Lake Hospital where Olivia worked in Admitting and Registration. "It's your daughter that's missing?"

"Yes." Olivia stepped forward, with Eve and Natalie right behind.

For the next five minutes they gave Tom Nicholls all the information he asked for. Natalie was also questioned, and then Nicholls got on the phone and fired off orders. A dozen more search parties were organized, and throughout, Olivia fought against the panic threatening to paralyze her. She very nearly gave in to it when she wanted to join one of the search parties and Nicholls wouldn't let her.

"You need to be at the security tent," he said. "That's going to be our command post and where Thea will be brought when she's found. And she'll need you then. You can't be off somewhere searching." Without waiting for her to protest, he beckoned to another officer. "Officer Wilkins here will take you to the security tent."

"I'll go and tell your mom and the others what's happening. Then I'll find you," Eve said, giving her a quick hug. "It's going to be okay, sweetie. I love you."

Olivia bit back her tears and allowed herself to be led off. She couldn't help remembering how, the night before, her last thought before going to bed had been about how much fun today was going to be.

What a fool she was.

She had tempted fate.

And now fate was showing her, once again, that she had no control over anything.

Chapter Two

Matthew Lawrence Britton wondered for about the thousandth time if he really *did* want to run for the US House of Representatives. He'd been greeting possible supporters at the festival for less than two hours, and he was already sick of it. And the election he was aiming for was more than two years away! He hated having to ask people for money, but without money—big money—no one, no matter what your name was, had a chance of winning an important election anymore.

Even more to the point, and the main thing that had been bothering him, was the fact he enjoyed his job as an assistant criminal district attorney for Hays County. And he was good at it. He might even have a shot at district attorney when his boss retired—something that was rumored to happen fairly soon.

But everyone, friends and family alike, seemed to think a more national stage was the road he should take.

They had been pressuring him for a while now, ever since the idea had been floated by an influential former law professor of his. Even his sister-in-law, Olivia, had weighed in, saying he'd make a wonderful representative for their district. He guessed he'd better make a final decision soon.

With all this on his mind, he was just about to approach Wylie Sheridan, an old family friend, when the loudspeakers dotted around the festival grounds crackled to life.

"This is an emergency message. May I have your attention, everyone?" boomed an authoritative male voice. "We have a missing child. Four-year-old Thea Britton has been separated from her family. Thea has curly blond hair and brown eyes. She's wearing blue denim pants, red sneakers, and a red-and-white-striped long-sleeved T-shirt and has a red bow in her hair. If anyone sees her now or remembers seeing her recently, please come to the security tent next to the main pavilion or call this number." He went on to give the number, then say that Thea had last been seen by the funnel cake booth. "She may have been chasing after a cat or kitten."

Matt had his phone out and had pressed Olivia's cell phone number before the announcement was finished. Thea was Matt's godchild, and even if she hadn't been the daughter of his late brother, Mark, Matt would have loved her. Thea was special—smart and sweet, loving and beautiful.

Just like her mother.

The thought, which had come more and more often lately, still had the power to make him feel guilty. He knew this emotion was ridiculous. Mark was gone. And he would have been the first to want Matt to take care of Olivia. Wouldn't he?

"Olivia?" Matt said when she answered. "I just heard the announcement about Thea. Where are you?"

"I'm at the security tent. The police want me to st-stay here." Her voice broke in a sob. "Oh, Matt, I'm so scared. She was right *there*, then she just *disappeared*!"

"I'm coming. I'll be there in two minutes." He was already running, his heart racing along with his feet. "It'll be okay. We'll find her."

When he reached the security tent, Olivia was pacing outside the door. She looked so forlorn, and so beautiful. Without thinking whether he should or shouldn't, he pulled her into his arms. Her slight body trembled, and more than anything, he wished he could tell her how he felt about her, how much he wanted to take care of her.

But this wasn't the time…or the place. And even if it was, he had no idea how she would react to this kind of declaration. He refused to think what he'd do if he confessed his feelings and she shot him down. Once he'd put those feelings into words, he knew they could never go back to their present relationship of caring brother-in-law to his brother's widow.

"Matt, oh, Matt," she sobbed. "I'm so afraid. The woods, the river, the lake. Who knows how far she's gone? You know how she is. How she always wants to investigate things. The questions she asks. What if…if someone…took her? But the police… I—I wanted to look for her, too, but they said I needed to stay here." Her body shuddered.

Matt inhaled the subtle fragrance of her silky hair as he held her and said over and over, "They'll find her. You've got everybody looking. They'll find her." But his mind was whirling as he imagined all the things that could have happened to Thea. He loved her as much as he had finally admitted—to himself if to no one else—he loved her mother.

Sometimes he wondered if he had always loved Olivia. Always wanted her. There was something about her that had touched him from the moment he was introduced to her when she and Mark were dating. Matt had always championed the underdog; it was simply part of his nature, and Olivia—in terms of how his parents viewed her, anyway—was definitely the underdog.

Matt's mother, in particular, disliked her daughter-in-law intensely and criticized her constantly: she wasn't raising their granddaughter to the standards of a Britton; she plopped the child in day care instead of allowing Vivienne to hire a nanny and have Thea raised in her grandparents' home under proper guidance and supervision; and worst of all, Vivienne considered Olivia to be one of the major reasons Mark was killed—because, in Vivienne's view—Olivia wasn't the wife he needed and kept him distracted and worried about his family instead of focusing on his job as a Black Hawk pilot. Unsaid was her bitter disappointment that the son she had imagined doing great things after fulfilling his service to his country, the son she'd envisioned going up the political ladder to high office, possibly the *highest* office, was gone forever. Olivia had been, and still was, a convenient scapegoat.

Matt's father was more tolerant than his wife and might have been okay with Olivia's entrance into the Britton family, but Vivienne ruled in the elder Brittons' home, and it was always easier for her husband to keep the peace and just go along. Actually, if Matt were being really honest with himself, he'd admit he'd long known his father was weak. That as long as he was able to live his privileged life, he didn't seem to care how that life was obtained or maintained.

Olivia finally withdrew from Matt's embrace and raised her tear-stained face to look at him. Her soft brown eyes met his. "I'm so glad you're here. I—I thought about calling you, but in all the confu—"

"It's okay. I know. C'mon, let's go sit down." He gestured to a nearby bench. When she hesitated, glancing back at the security tent, he said, "Don't worry. I'll let them know you're right here. If they want you, they'll come out and get you."

For the next hour, both Matt and her cousin Eve tried to keep Olivia calm as people came and went, as the security team and the police department officers combined their efforts and the search parties combed the nearby grounds and questioned dozens of people.

Olivia eventually just looked numb. Her eyes clouded with worry and fear, she kept biting her bottom lip and twisting her hands. She couldn't sit still, and every ten minutes or so she'd jump up and start pacing again. Or her phone would ring and she'd either talk or she'd say, "I can't talk! I have to keep the line clear in case..." Then her voice would trail off and she'd have to sit down again.

Matt and Eve, whom he'd met several times—and liked very much—exchanged a lot of concerned looks. He knew what Eve was thinking, because he was thinking it, too. The longer it took the searchers to find Thea, the more likely it was the outcome of the searching wouldn't be good. His own fear felt like a huge weight in his chest, and it was all he could do to keep that fear from showing.

Olivia needed him...and Eve...to be strong.

He thought about calling his parents, but he didn't.

The last thing Olivia needed was for his mother to come charging over to the festival with her accusations and criticisms.

But after more than two hours had gone by, and one by one the search teams reported in with no success, Matt knew he could no longer delay notifying his parents. He waited until Olivia was busy with Officer Nicholls, and then he walked a few feet away and placed the call.

His mother answered. "Hello, Matthew," she said. "To what do I owe this pleasure?"

Matt gritted his teeth at this subtle dig. She never missed a chance to let him know he wasn't living up to her expectations. "Listen, Mom. I need to tell you something. Now, don't get hysterical, but I'm at the festival, and... Thea is missing. The police are here, and—"

"I see," his mother said, interrupting. "And just how did *that* happen? Just exactly how did my granddaughter go missing?"

Matt blinked. What was wrong with his mother? She didn't sound the least bit upset, just disdainful.

"What happened is," he said in the most measured tone he could manage, "Olivia's family is here celebrating her mother's birthday, and her mother felt sick and fainted, and in all the commotion, Thea wandered off. The authorities organized search parties, but they haven't found—"

"Of course they haven't found her."

"What the *hell*?" Matt said, losing his temper. "Aren't you even *upset*? Your only grandchild is missing and all you can do is imply the security people, the police, aren't doing their—"

"Do not swear at me, Matthew," she said, interrupting him again. "I'm not upset because Thea is here."

"She's *what*?"

"You heard me. She's here. Where she *should* be. Safe and sound. More than I can say for when she's in her so-called mother's so-called care."

If his mother had been physically in his presence, Matt knew he might have choked her, he was that angry. "And just how did she happen to be there? Did someone find her and bring her to you?"

"I found her. I was at the festival myself, earlier, and I saw her wandering all alone, that *family* of her mother's nowhere to be seen, so I did what any grandmother would do. I scooped her up and I brought her home. She's even now upstairs playing happily in the nursery. In fact, I can hear her talking. I think she's on Buddy Boy." Buddy Boy was the name of the rocking horse that had been in Vivienne's family since *she* was a child. "You know how she loves Buddy Boy and how she talks to him, just like her father did when he was a boy. Now if you'll excuse me, I must get back—"

"I'll be there in fifteen minutes," Matt said, doing his own interrupting now. His heart was once again hammering, but not in fear this time. He felt murderous rage, mixed with disbelief. How could his mother be so downright cruel? He was appalled by Vivienne's behavior and the way she had so callously disregarded the fear and worry Olivia and her family were feeling. Hell, that *he'd* been feeling! And all those people who had been searching for hours. The police, the security people…it all boggled his mind.

He disconnected the call and strode to where Olivia was still talking to Tom Nicholls. "Call off the search party," he told Tom. "Thea's been found. She's at my mother's."

Ignoring Nicholls's startled expression and the inevitable questions, Matt took Olivia's arm and said, "C'mon, let's go get her. I'll explain everything on the way."

Eve, who had heard the exchange, met Matt's eyes. She looked stunned, but didn't say anything.

"She'll call you, or I will, after we get Thea," he said. "Tell the others."

Eve nodded and Matt knew she'd take care of things there.

"Where'd you park?" Olivia asked, her face beginning to portray her conflicting emotions. Matt still found it hard to believe his mother had done this unspeakable thing. To take Thea home and never call Olivia to tell her where Thea was defied every standard of decent behavior. He'd always known how manipulative and controlling his mother was—and how insensitive to the feelings of others when they interfered with what she wanted—but he'd never imagined she was actually heartless and devoid of compassion for a fellow human being.

"On Waterside," he said. "This way." Grabbing Olivia's hand, he led her through the crowd and together, they hurried to where his BMW was parked. He hit his remote, the doors unlocked, and Olivia was in the passenger seat before he could even think of helping her. In minutes, they were on their way.

As he drove, he quickly told her a sanitized version of his conversation with his mother. From the way Olivia's throat worked, he knew what she must be feeling, yet all she said was, "I don't really care why your mother did what she did...or what she said. I'm just thankful Thea is okay. And I just want to get her and take her home."

"I know." But he also knew when she'd had time to really think about this, Olivia would feel differently. In fact, he wouldn't be surprised if she ended up forbidding his mother to see Thea again. Hell, if he was in Olivia's shoes, he might consider moving away from Crandall Lake to put as much distance between her and his mother as she could.

Even the thought that Olivia might move away made him want to do something terrible to his mother.

Barely twelve minutes had elapsed since his phone conversation with Vivienne before Matt and Olivia were pulling into the long drive leading to his parents' stately home. Matt parked in the front turnaround, and again Olivia was out of the car and dashing up the shallow front steps before he managed to get out himself.

Olivia jabbed at the doorbell, but Matt, who had a key to the house, shoved it into the lock and opened the door himself. The first thing he saw was his mother, looking coolly elegant in tailored black pants paired with a black-and-white geometric top, her expertly colored blond hair in a chin-length style she'd recently adopted. Vivienne was halfway down the curving staircase that led to the second floor. She stopped at their entrance and lifted her head defiantly. Her blue eyes met Matt's. She ignored Olivia.

"I've come for my daughter," Olivia said, her voice only betraying a tiny tremor.

Vivienne turned her icy glare to Olivia. "You're wasting your time, because I won't allow you to take her. It's quite obvious she's not safe with you, and I can't have you putting her in danger again."

Matt attempted to interrupt her, but she ignored him and kept going. "I'm not surprised, though. I've always known you weren't a fit mother. You're just lucky I'm the one who found her. That some crazy person didn't abduct her."

"Mother—" Matt stopped, took a deep breath to keep

his voice calm in case they could be heard upstairs. "You can't keep Thea here. Olivia is her mother, and she has every right to take Thea home with her. Now before—"

"Before *what*?" his mother said, her voice rising a notch. "Are you going to physically manhandle me? Threaten me? Your own *mother*? You'd better be careful, Matthew, or I will—"

Before Vivienne could finish her sentence, Olivia ran to the stairway and pushed past his mother, nearly causing Vivienne to lose her balance, but she managed to grab the banister in time. Matt didn't hesitate. He, too, went up the stairs, taking them two at a time. He didn't look at his mother as he passed her. He didn't trust himself. He couldn't remember ever being this angry.

Olivia had already entered the old nursery where both he and Mark, as well as their younger sister, Madeleine, had spent the major part of their childhood. By the time Matt caught up, he sensed rather than saw his mother a few feet behind him.

Amelia, who had been the Britton family housekeeper since before Matt was born, sat in a child-sized chair as she watched Thea, sitting across from her, happily putting together a puzzle. "I'm sorry, Mr. Matt," Amelia said, looking up as he entered the room. "But she wouldn't listen to me when I told your mother she should call Miss Olivia."

"I know this isn't your fault," Matt said as Olivia, with a cry, ran to Thea. She picked her up and kissed her over and over again.

"Mommy! Stop!" Thea said, looking at Matt. "Unca Matt!" She tried to squirm out of her mother's grasp, raising her arms to Matt.

"Oh, sweetheart! I thought you were lost," Olivia said. "I'm just so happy you're not."

"I wasn't lost. Mimi found me." *Mimi* was the pet name Vivienne had insisted Thea call her, saying the title of grandmother implied she was old. Matt had rolled his eyes when he heard that one.

"Good. I must thank Mimi," Olivia said, still hugging Thea.

"Mommy, let me down," Thea said again.

"We're taking her home now," Matt said to his mother, who stood behind him.

"You're going to be sorry for this," Vivienne muttered under her breath.

Matt knew she was keeping her voice down because she didn't want to make a scene in front of Thea. Nor did he, and he knew Olivia felt the same way. They might have their issues with his mother, and she might be extremely misguided, but she was still Thea's grandmother, and Thea loved her Mimi and Poppa.

"Mommy!" Thea shouted. "I said I want Unca Matt!"

Olivia, meeting Matt's eyes, finally let Thea loose, and she ran into his arms. Matt picked her up and held her close. Laughing, she wrapped her little arms around him and snuggled in. If someone had asked Matt how he felt at this moment, he wasn't sure he would have been able to put his emotions into words. His heart was too full. Right here in this room were the two people in the world who meant the most to him, and somehow, some way, he had to figure out how to keep them both safe forever. But at the present moment, he just needed to get them out of here.

"Where's Dad?" he asked his mother as he motioned for Olivia to precede him out of the room.

"Playing golf," his mother said coldly. "Where else?"

"Tell him I'll call him later."

When she didn't answer, just gave him another icy stare, then turned and walked down the hall toward her bedroom, he sighed and followed Olivia down the stairs and out to the car.

As Matt drove Olivia and Thea back to the festival to pick up Olivia's car, he apologized in an undertone for the things his mother had said.

"Forget it," she said. "Thea is safe, I have her back, and that's all that counts."

That was the most important thing, yes, but Matt knew there were going to be repercussions to this episode. However, no matter what it cost him, he'd already decided he'd do everything in his power to make sure none of those repercussions affected Olivia. The guilt for this debacle lay at one door, and that door wasn't hers.

When they reached Olivia's car, she thanked him. "I don't know what I'd've done if you hadn't been with me today. I—I would have put off calling your mother because…" Her voice trailed off.

"I know." He wondered how long his mother would have kept Thea without notifying Olivia. He wanted to think she would have relented and done the decent thing, yet would she? Surely, when his father arrived home she would have had to tell him what she'd done.

But maybe not. Maybe she'd have made up some story and his father would have been none the wiser. It wasn't as if Thea had never spent the night with his parents. Olivia had been generous, even when his mother had not. That quality—Olivia's generosity—was one of the many things about her he'd grown to admire.

"I'll always be there for you and Thea, Olivia," he said, reaching out and squeezing her shoulder.

That brought a smile to her face. "Thanks, Matt. Eve said something similar last night. I'm lucky to have you guys, I know that."

Not that lucky, he thought. But he smiled, too. "That's the Olivia I know. A glass half-full girl."

"Yeah, that's me. A cockeyed optimist."

"Nothing wrong with that."

"Mommy, put me down," Thea said, struggling to get out of Olivia's arms once again.

"Thea, you know you have to be belted into your seat," Olivia said. "So you can be safe, and we can go home."

"I don't wanna go home. I wanna go back to the fes-table. With Unca Matt."

"Festival," Olivia said.

"That's what I said! Festable!"

Matt wanted to laugh. Thea might be sweet and loving most of the time, but she was also a very bright, very determined and very stubborn four-year-old with definite opinions of her own. "I'm not going back to the festival, honey. I'm going home and you're going home, too, because your Grammy and Aunt Stella and everyone is waiting for you. I think you're having birthday cake, right?"

"Uncle Matt's right," Olivia said. "Grammy will need help blowing out her candles."

"Candles!" Thea said with a delighted smile, obviously forgetting all about the festival. "Presents, too?"

"Yes, presents, too," Olivia said.

"For me!"

"No, honey, not for you. You're not the birthday girl today. Grammy is."

Thea gave her mother a look that said that didn't seem fair. "Unca Matt's coming, too."

"No, sweetheart, I can't." He wanted to say he hadn't been invited, but he knew that wasn't fair. He'd be putting Olivia on the spot.

Thea looked as if she was going to protest that, too, but she didn't, and finally allowed Matt to get her buckled into her seat and kissed him goodbye.

Once Thea was safely settled in her Camry, Olivia turned to him. "Thanks, again, Matt." She lowered her voice. "Do I need to call anyone, do you think? Like Chief Donnelly? Apologize for everything?"

Barton Donnelly, the chief of police in Crandall Lake, was a crony of Matt's father. Matt would be sure to apprise him of what had actually happened. No way was he letting Olivia take the fall for any of this. "I'll take care of it," he assured her. "Don't worry. Just enjoy the rest of the weekend with your family, and we'll talk tomorrow night after Eve's gone. She *is* leaving tomorrow, right?"

"That's the plan," Olivia said. "Luckily for her, she has her husband's plane and pilot at her disposal."

Matt could see the weariness returning to Olivia's face. The stress of everything that had happened today had exhausted her. He gave her a quick hug, careful to make it brotherly and not lover-like, then stood watching as she walked around to the passenger side of her car, got in and drove away.

As always, when they parted company, the world seemed less bright with her gone. If only he could always be there for her in the way he wanted to be, but if today had shown him anything, it had shown him how hopeless his situation actually was. For even if Olivia should ever feel the same way about him that he felt about her, the only way they could ever be together would be for him to break all ties with his family, and for him and Olivia and Thea to leave Crandall Lake behind forever.

And that was impossible.

For them…and for him.

Wasn't it?

Chapter Three

Olivia wasn't quite as forgiving as she had pretended to be. She just hadn't wanted to cause any more trouble between Matt and his mother. Because if Matt kept siding with her against his mother, things would only get worse. His parents weren't just Thea's grandparents. They were one of the most influential couples in the state.

Hugh Britton was the president of a large commercial real estate and investment firm Vivienne's great-grandfather had founded, and the family owned thousands of acres of property around Texas and parts of Oklahoma, including the oil and mineral rights in places that continued to add to the family coffers. The Britton family influence was vast, their resources unlimited, and Olivia, no matter how angry and upset she was over what Vivienne had done today, did not want to worsen an already touchy situation.

In addition, even though she hadn't admitted this to anyone, including Eve, Olivia had begun to have feelings for Matt—feelings that extended beyond those of family ties. She knew it was unwise, she knew what she felt for him could never go anywhere—in fact, he could never even *know*—but she couldn't seem to help herself. More than any other member of Mark's family, she had been drawn to Matt from the first day they'd met. Perhaps it was because he was so kind and welcoming, such a contrast to his mother. As she'd gotten to know him better, she'd realized he was a genuinely good man and well respected, in addition to being handsome and smart and fun to be with. She didn't know exactly what it was about him that drew her. All she knew was, the admiration and connection she'd felt for him as her brother-in-law had morphed into something else in the last year.

So the last thing she wanted was to cause any problems for him. It was bad enough he had helped her today. Vivienne would probably make his life hell because of it.

Oh, Matt, why can't we just be two normal people? Why do we have to have this complicated relationship that spells only trouble for us?

This question…and more…lay heavy on her mind as she called Eve to tell her they were on their way.

"We're at your mom's house, waiting," Eve said.

"Be there in ten."

"Is everything okay?"

Olivia sighed. "We'll talk later."

When Olivia pulled into the driveway at her mother's house, Eve and the twins were waiting on the front porch. The cousins exchanged looks as the twins boisterously greeted Thea.

"I'll tell you everything tonight," Olivia murmured as the screen door opened and the rest of the family emerged. While her mother, Eve's mother and Stella hugged and kissed Thea and told her not to ever scare them like that again, Eve just watched and smiled. But she covertly took Olivia's hand and gave it a comforting squeeze.

"So I guess this was all a big misunderstanding?" Eve's mother said carefully.

"Yes," Olivia said in an equally even tone, "Thea's Mimi couldn't find us, so she made sure Thea was safe, didn't she, sweetheart?"

Thea nodded happily. "Mimi said you wouldn't care, Mommy."

"Well, I did care, and I was worried because Mimi didn't call me, but I'm just glad you're okay. We all are."

Olivia knew they all understood what she wouldn't say in front of the children, so the subject was dropped, and the matter of the birthday cake and presents were introduced, much to the excitement of Thea. The twins gamely joined in the fun, and Olivia was able, for a little while at least, to relax and just enjoy being with the people she loved most in the world.

Like Thea, she did wish Matt could be there, though. She wished she could have invited him, but her family, especially Eve, were too sharp, too aware of Olivia and her emotions, especially since Mark's death. It was hard enough to keep the right tone and distance when it was just the two cousins together, but Matt amongst her family? Olivia was afraid she'd somehow give herself away. And having her family know how she felt about Matt would make a tough situation impossible.

"Auntie Norma, Mom said this is a special birthday," Natalie said after the cake and ice cream had been consumed and Norma was preparing to open her gifts.

Olivia's mother beamed. "It is. It's my social security birthday, so I can retire now, if I want to."

"You mean from your job at Dr. Ross's?" asked Nathan. Dr. Ross was a popular veterinarian in Crandall Lake, and Norma was his office manager.

"Yes," Norma answered.

"Are you going to, Grandma?" Natalie persisted.

"I don't think so. Not yet, anyway," Olivia's mother said. She grinned. "I like my job. I'd miss the animals."

Nathan nodded. "I thought so. And Grumpy would miss *you*."

They all laughed, agreeing. Grumpy was a rescue cat Dr. Ross had adopted, and he'd turned into the office mascot, living there 24/7. All the pet owners who visited the office enjoyed Grumpy.

Olivia hoped her mother stuck to that decision. Sixty-seven was too young to retire nowadays. Plus it wasn't as if her mother was wealthy. She had some savings, Olivia knew, and some insurance money left from when Olivia's dad died, but her mother could live another twenty years…or longer. No, it was better if her mother stayed on the job as long as she could, and not just because of finances. Everything Olivia knew from her hospital job showed that remaining engaged and active was good for older people, that they lived longer and healthier lives because of it.

Olivia continued to think about her mother while Norma opened her presents. When she finished, it was time to gather everyone and head for home.

"Will we see you at church in the morning?" Eve's mother asked as Olivia, Eve and the children said their goodbyes.

After agreeing they would, the cousins took their leave and headed for Olivia's house, just minutes away.

It took nearly forty minutes, but finally the twins and Thea were settled in the living room with the movie *Frozen*, although Nathan was also playing a game on his iPad. Olivia and Eve headed for the kitchen, where Olivia put the kettle on so they could have tea.

"Tell me everything," Eve said quietly.

So Olivia did. By the time their tea was ready, she'd finished with her blow-by-blow account of the scene at the elder Brittons' home.

"She's unbelievable," Eve said, shaking her head. "I just don't know what she thought she was accomplishing by keeping Thea there and not telling you."

"With her twisted logic, she probably thought she was reinforcing her belief that I'm an unfit mother."

"Doesn't she realize you could keep her from seeing Thea *at all*?"

Olivia shrugged. "She probably knows I wouldn't do that unless there was no other alternative."

"But why not?" Eve said. Her blue eyes flashed with anger as she stirred milk into her tea.

"Oh, Eve," Olivia said resignedly, "you know why not. If I tried to keep Vivienne away from Thea, she'd make a world of trouble for me." She drank some of her tea. "I just… Life can be hard enough. I can't deal with constant stress and all the drama that comes with any conflict with my mother-in-law."

"So you're just going to ignore what she did today? Listen, why don't I ask Austin to—"

"No! You're not going to ask Austin to do anything. Matt said he'd take care of things…talk to his dad and to Chief Donnelly."

"Yes, but that's just today. What about tomorrow?

What about next week? What about *you*? What if this vendetta against you escalates? She seems to be capable of anything!"

Olivia rubbed her forehead. "Eve, please. Can we talk about something else? I'm so tired of thinking about Vivienne."

Eve looked as if she wanted to protest, but all she did was sigh and give Olivia a reluctant nod. "Okay. I'm sorry. I just…well, I hate this for you. After all you've been through, it sucks."

"I know you worry about me, and I love you for it." Olivia smiled at her cousin and thought about how grateful she was that Eve was here today.

"I want you to promise me something, though," Eve said.

"What?" Olivia said warily.

"If she tries anything else, *anything*, you'll call me immediately. Okay?"

Olivia shook her head. "Eve, what can you do about it? You'll be a thousand miles or more away."

"Just promise."

"Oh, all right, I promise."

"Good." Eve's eyes narrowed. "I'm not without resources, either, you know. As Queen Vivienne will soon find out if she messes with you again."

On that note, the conversation turned to Olivia's mother, then to what the cousins might feed their offspring…and themselves…for dinner. Soon Olivia was laughing and had managed to temporarily wipe Vivienne out of her mind.

But down deep, she knew Vivienne would always be a threat to her peaceful existence with her daughter.

And unfortunately, for now at least, there wasn't a thing Olivia could do about it.

* * *

Matt decided golf game or no golf game, he would try to reach his father on his cell phone.

His dad answered almost immediately. "What is it, Matt? I'm playing golf."

"I know that, Dad. Just wondered when you'd be finished."

"I don't know. Around five, I guess."

"Can we meet for a drink before you go home? I need to talk to you."

"Can't you just come to the house?"

"No. I'll explain later."

Matt heard his father sigh. "Where do you want to meet?"

"How about The Grill?" He'd named a popular restaurant and bar near the golf course.

"I'll call you when I finish here," his father said.

"All right."

Good, Matt thought as they hung up. He wanted to be the first to tell his father what had transpired today. Certainly before his mother got a chance to, since she would spin the story in her favor. Even so, Matt knew his father was too smart not to realize Vivienne's stories were *always* spun in her favor.

Matt had tolerated the way his mother treated Olivia because he'd known any interference would only make Vivienne more vindictive toward her daughter-in-law. But today's debacle had changed something in the way Matt saw things. Something had to be done before his mother escalated to something even worse than she'd done today. And the only way anything *could* be done was if he could somehow persuade his father to join him and unite against her.

Would his father go along with that?

Matt would just have to wait and see.

* * *

Vivienne was furious. How dare Matthew take that woman's side against his own mother? The fact Olivia wasn't fit to raise a Britton grandchild was indisputable—anyone with any sense could see it—especially after what had happened today. Yet Vivienne's own son refused to see the truth. Vivienne gritted her teeth. She could just scream.

Matthew had always taken Olivia's side, from the very beginning when Mark brought her home to meet them. Vivienne had seen through the girl immediately. A wannabe. Someone not fit to shine the shoes of her youngest son, let alone marry him. But neither Mark nor Matthew would listen to her. And now look where they all were. Her beautiful Mark was dead, struck down before he'd had any chance of showing the world how special he was. And her willful oldest son—who really couldn't hold a candle to Mark—was still defending Olivia.

Well, Vivienne had warned him. And he'd ignored the warning. Matthew would be sorry. Very sorry. Did he really think he could get elected to the US House of Representatives without his parents' support? If he did, he was going to be sorely disappointed, because it wasn't possible. All Vivienne had to do was talk to a few people, drop a few hints that Matthew would not have his parents or his parents' money behind him, and the race would be over before it ever began.

Did he think she *wouldn't* oppose him? Ha. He had another think coming. She would not only oppose him, she would actively work to see he was defeated by openly and financially backing his opponent, whomever that turned out to be.

Not only that, she would make sure both her and

Hugh's wills were changed. They'd been changed once, right after Mark married that...*woman*...and they could be changed again. *Would* be changed again, because Hugh would do whatever she told him to do. He liked his easy, no-questions-asked life too much to buck her, not when she and she alone controlled the purse strings.

And...if Matthew changed paths and decided not to run for the House but instead to go for the district attorney's slot when Carter Davis retired...well, Vivienne would have something to say about that, too. No one, absolutely no one, opposed Vivienne Marchand Britton and survived to tell about it.

It was exactly five fifteen when Matt's cell rang.

"Matt?"

"Dad? You done?"

"Yes. I'll be at The Grill in about fifteen minutes."

"Okay. I'm leaving now, too."

Matt pulled into the parking lot of the restaurant just before his dad's Lexus. Getting out of his car, Matt walked over to meet his father.

At sixty-two years old, Hugh Britton looked a good ten years younger. Tall, tanned, still slender and fit, with a thick head of salt-and-pepper hair, he was the picture of health. Matt often wondered just how his dad had managed it, especially married to Matt's mother. Then again, Matt knew how. Hugh took the path of least resistance. As long as he could live the way he wanted to live and Matt's mother turned a blind eye to the other women Matt suspected his father of being involved with over the years, he didn't seem to care what she did.

"What's up, son?" Hugh said as they walked into the entrance to the bar side of the crowded place. "Problems with the campaign already?"

"No. Problems with Mom."

His father frowned. "Matt, you know I try to stay out of—"

"This isn't something you can ignore."

His father pointedly looked at his watch. "I only have about twenty minutes."

Matt waited until they were seated and had ordered their drinks before telling his father an abbreviated version of the story.

Hugh toyed with his drink. "Is Thea okay?"

"Thea's fine. She didn't even know anything was wrong."

"Well, then—" Hugh shrugged. "All's well that ends well."

Matt stared at his father. "All's well that *ends well*? Dad! Olivia was sick with worry. So was her family. And possibly a hundred other people, not to mention the police, were involved. This time, Mom's gone too far."

His father didn't meet his eyes.

After a few seconds of silence, Matt said, "Don't you think we need to do something? You know she won't listen to me, but can't you make Mom understand that she can't continue this vendetta against Olivia? You know, if Olivia wanted to, she could get a court order barring both of you from even *seeing* Thea. Any judge, hearing about today's incident, would be hard-pressed *not* to rule in Olivia's favor if she decided to go that route."

His father finally looked at him. "Would Olivia do that?"

"In her shoes, I would."

"You haven't suggested anything like that, have you?"

Matt shook his head. Not that he hadn't felt like it.

His father sighed heavily. Drank more of his Scotch.

Then turned worried eyes to Matt. "I just don't know what you want *me* to do."

"Confront Mom. Tell her you won't stand for any more of this unfair treatment of Olivia."

"Easier said than done," his father muttered.

"C'mon, Dad. Can't you at least *try*? Maybe if you tell her what could happen if she doesn't stop this behavior, she'll think twice next time she's tempted to do anything else."

His father still didn't look at him. "I can't promise anything, but I will try." So saying, he finished off his drink and looked around for their waiter. "I need to get going. Your mother will be upset if I don't get home soon. She said the Hoopers were coming for dinner, and I still have to shower and change."

Matt said he'd settle the bill and watched as his father left. A few minutes later, as Matt left, too, he didn't feel optimistic. Oh, he figured his father *would* try, but Matt could pretty much predict that his mother would roll right over Hugh and, ultimately, nothing would change.

Olivia and Eve and their children went to nine o'clock Mass at Saint Nick's, the church where they'd both made their First Holy Communion and their Confirmation. It was also the church where Eve and Bill Kelly, her first husband and the man who had raised the twins as his own, had been married, and where the twins and Thea had been baptized.

After Mass, Eve and the twins left to meet Austin Crenshaw for breakfast, while Olivia and Thea headed to the activity center where coffee, juice and doughnuts were being served. Once they got there, Olivia looked for her mom and Eve's mom.

"You know, honey," Olivia's mother said once they

were all seated at one of the tables, "I've been think-ing about what happened yesterday, and it really both-ers me."

Olivia shook her head in warning. "Little pitchers," she said under her breath.

"I just think you should do something about it."

"Mom…"

"Okay, fine. But let's talk later."

Olivia should have known her mother wouldn't be content to drop the subject. And, as it turned out, nei-ther was Eve. Later that day, after Olivia and Thea were back home and Eve and the twins had returned from their breakfast with Austin, Eve suggested they drop the children off at the local multiplex, where a new Disney film was showing. "We can sit in the food court while they're seeing the movie," she said, "have something to drink and be free to talk."

Olivia wasn't surprised to find Vivienne was the subject uppermost on Eve's mind.

"I can't go back to California unless I know you're going to be okay," she said once they were settled with Frappuccinos from Starbucks.

Olivia sighed. "Eve, please stop worrying. I can han-dle Vivienne. Haven't I *been* handling her for years now?"

"Seems to me her campaign against you is esca-lating. What she did yesterday is atrocious. And both your mom and mine agree with me. That woman is out of control."

"She does seem to be getting worse."

"At least Matt is on your side," Eve said. Then, shock-ing Olivia, she added, "You do know he's in love with you?"

Olivia stared at her. "That…that's crazy. He's just a friend. He's…he's Mark's *brother*!"

"So?" Eve said. "It's not like he's *your* brother."

"You're wrong," Olivia insisted. "He doesn't think of me that way." But inside, she was trembling. Did he? Was it possible?

"I'm not wrong, and you're blind. Actually, your mother agrees with me."

"My *mother*? When did you talk to her about this?"

"Yesterday, before you arrived at the house. She said she's been thinking this for a while now. My mother agreed."

"No. It's crazy."

"Why is it crazy?"

"Because…it just is. He…he's never acted like anything but my brother-in-law. Anyway, even if he *was* interested in me, in that way, it could never work out."

"And why not?"

"You know why not. One word. *Vivienne*."

Eve laughed. "Oh, Liv, think about it. It would be so perfect! I can't even imagine the look on her face if you and Matt should—"

"Stop it!" Olivia said. "Just stop it. Matt is *not* in love with me."

"Actually, I'd be surprised if he *wasn't* in love with you. After all, you're beautiful and smart and the two of you get along like a house afire. Plus, he adores Thea…"

Olivia scoffed. "Matt is around beautiful and accomplished women all the time. Much more beautiful and accomplished than *me*." She couldn't help but think of Jenna Forrester, a fellow attorney whom Matt had dated for nearly a year until their breakup in the summer. Jenna was gorgeous!

"Why are you constantly putting yourself down?" Eve persisted.

"I'm not. I'm...just being realistic."

"Uh-huh, just like you were being realistic when you said Austin wasn't interested in you. And you were totally wrong there, too."

"What do you mean? Did you *say* something to Austin today? Eve, you promised you wouldn't."

"I promised I wouldn't mention you were ready to date again. I did not promise I wouldn't even mention your name."

Olivia closed her eyes. What had Eve said?

Eve started to laugh. "Come on, Liv. It's no big deal. I didn't say anything other than telling him what happened at the festival."

"You told him *that*?"

"Why not? It isn't as if no one else knows. There must have been a hundred people involved in looking for Thea."

"I know, but—"

"Don't you want to know what he said?"

Olivia sighed. "What did he say?"

"He said if you have any more trouble with Vivienne— anything at all—to call him. He said he would be happy to represent you, if it ever came to that."

"Why would he say *that*?"

"Why?" Eve said. "Because he's a nice guy."

"No, that's not what I meant. Did you somehow *suggest* I might take legal action against Vivienne?"

"Liv, you know I wouldn't do that. It's just that he's a lawyer. That's the way lawyers think." Eve smiled. "He also asked if you were dating anyone."

"Really?"

"Really."

"What did you tell him?"

"I told him you hadn't been, but I thought you might be ready."

Olivia guessed she couldn't be mad at Eve for that. But still, she felt uncomfortable.

"Don't you want to know his reaction to that?"

Olivia rolled her eyes. "Whether I do or not, I'm sure you're going to tell me."

"He asked me if I thought you'd go out with him." Eve grinned. "See? I told you he was interested in you."

Olivia wasn't sure what to think. "And what did you say?"

"I told him I didn't know, that he'd have to call you and find out on his own."

Olivia had begun to feel as if everyone, Eve included, was pushing her in a direction she wasn't sure she wanted to go. Unfortunately, she also didn't know how to stop this momentum.

"What's wrong now?" Eve said.

"Nothing."

"Look, no one's forcing you to do anything. If you don't want to go out with Austin, just say no when he asks."

Olivia bit her lip.

Eve frowned. "What?"

"I don't know. I guess I'm just feeling a bit pressured."

Eve threw up her hands. "I don't understand you, Liv. What's the problem? Honestly, I don't care if you go out with Austin...or anyone, for that matter. I just thought that's what you wanted."

She hadn't said, *make up your mind*, but Olivia knew that's what Eve thought. And actually, she'd have a right to feel that way. Because Olivia *had* been blowing hot and cold. Trouble was, she just wasn't comfortable moving back into the world of dating. In fact, it scared the you-know-what out of her to even contemplate dating again.

She made a face. "I'm sorry, Eve. You're right. And I'm not mad at you or anything. I guess I have to make up my mind what it is I really want right now."

"Yeah, you do."

Olivia took a deep breath. "And I will."

"Good. And, Liv…"

"What?"

"Austin's a good guy. You could do a lot worse."

"I know."

"But if you decide you're not interested in him, it's okay. I won't be upset with you. Just…be nice. Let him down gently."

"I promise I will."

"Okay, good." Eve looked at her watch. "And now I think it's about time to go get our kiddos."

As the cousins headed toward the theater, Olivia's thoughts were all over the place, and she wasn't sure about much. But one thing she *was* sure about was how her life was changing, whether she wanted it to or not.

Chapter Four

"Mommy?"

"Yes, sweetie?" Olivia finished tucking Thea into bed. Eve and the twins had left for home earlier, and Olivia had just finished giving Thea her bath.

"Nathan and Natalie have two daddies." She pronounced Natalie's name "Natlee."

Gazing down into her daughter's brown eyes, Olivia felt her heart swell with love. "I know."

Thea's forehead knitted in thought. "Why do they?"

Olivia sat on the side of the bed and took Thea's hand. "I explained that to you, honey. It's because their daddy Bill married someone else and now their mommy is married to their daddy Adam." Olivia had decided this was the only explanation Thea could understand right now. When she got older, Olivia would explain the situation properly.

Thea thought about this for a few minutes, then said, "My daddy died."

Olivia swallowed. "Yes, he did."

"But he loved me a lot."

"Yes, honey, he did. Your daddy loved you so much."

"Mommy, tell me the story about my daddy."

By now Olivia had to blink back tears, but she managed to keep it together and launch into the familiar story of the handsome daddy who was very brave and very strong and who had loved his little girl more than anyone else in the world. "And your daddy is now watching over you from Heaven," she finished with a tender smile.

"He's my garden angel," Thea said, beginning the ritual that always followed the "daddy story."

"Yes, he's your guardian angel."

"And he'll always keep me safe."

"Always."

"I have his hair." Thea touched her golden curls.

"You do."

"And his nose." Now Thea was giggling, pointing at and mashing down her nose.

"Except it's not as big," Olivia said, laughing in spite of the lump in her throat.

"And his ears!" Thea tugged at both her ears.

"Except they're not as big, either."

"If he was here, he'd smother me with kisses!" Thea exclaimed, an expression of delight already on her face as she waited for what was coming.

Olivia drew back. "I'm his messenger. Ready or not, here they come." Then, with an exaggerated laugh, pretending to be a dive-bomber, she buried her face in her daughter's warm neck and began kissing her.

"Mommy, that tickles!"

Olivia finished by kissing the tip of Thea's nose and murmuring, "Good night, sweetheart."

Thea sighed happily. "Good night, Mommy."

"And good night to Daddy…" Olivia began.

"Up in Heaven," Thea finished.

Olivia got up and dimmed the carousel lamp on Thea's dresser. She stood there for a long moment watching her child drift into sleep. Then, whispering softly, "Sweet dreams, my beautiful girl," she left Thea's bedroom and headed downstairs.

Matt waited until nine thirty Sunday night before calling Olivia. He knew Thea's bedtime was normally at eight, but figured he'd give Olivia some time to un-wind from her hectic and emotionally chaotic week-end before fulfilling his promise to check in with her.

"How are you?" he asked when she answered.

"I'm okay."

But he could tell just by her tone that she wasn't okay. He wasn't surprised. Olivia was strong, much tougher than his mother imagined, but she was only human. It would be hard *not* to be affected by the treatment his mother had dished out.

"Eve and the kids get off okay?"

"Right on time. She was anxious to get back to Adam. Newlyweds, you know."

In her voice, he heard many things, and he knew she was already missing Eve, but more than that, there was a deeper sadness. "What's wrong, Olivia? Did some-thing else happen since I saw you? Or are you thinking about my mother and what she did?"

Silence greeted his question, followed by a barely perceptible sigh. Just when he thought she wasn't going to answer at all, she said softly, "When I was putting Thea to bed, she asked me why Natalie and Nathan have two daddies."

The words, filled with pain, hit Matt somewhere in the vicinity of his solar plexus. He didn't know what to say. Groping clumsily, he finally said, "Life sucks sometimes."

"Yes," Olivia said in a weary voice.

"Liv, do you want—"

"You know what," she said before he could finish his half-assed question, "I can't talk about this right now. I'm so tired. I just want to go to bed. I'm sorry, Matt. I'll call you tomorrow."

And then she was gone.

Matt sat staring into space for a long time after that disconnect. Two emotions were warring inside. The first was anger at his mother and the second was the fierce love he felt for Olivia and Thea.

When he finally got up and went into the compact kitchen of his mid-rise condo near the county offices where he spent most of his waking hours, he had made up his mind. No matter what the outcome of his father's attempt to talk some sense into his mother, Matt would do whatever it took to protect Olivia and Thea from any more pain…or loss. And if that meant a complete break from his family, so be it.

Olivia had a hard time falling asleep. She kept thinking about Thea and reliving the day she'd gotten the news about Mark and his death. She'd thought she was recovered from his loss, and had accepted what had happened. She'd believed she was fully ready to move forward.

But tonight's bedtime ritual with Thea, always bittersweet, had been more painful, more filled with an almost overwhelming sense of loss. Was it always going to be this way? Would she never be able to feel entirely happy again?

Of course, you'll move forward. Of course you won't always be sad. This is a normal progression of grief you're feeling. Remember how you felt when your dad died? Magnify that by about ten, and that's what you're dealing with now. When you lose someone you love, it's always two steps forward, one step back.

The voice in her head wasn't hers. It was Eve's. And Olivia's head knew Eve was right. But her heart was having a hard time tonight.

That's because Thea showed you a part of her heart. We can always deal with our own sorrows and regrets, but when it comes to our children, it's tougher. We want to protect them from everything. And we can't.

Eve again.

Olivia almost laughed. Eve was like her alter ego or something. Or her twin. They just understood each other.

Eve was right. Olivia needed to quit beating herself up because she'd taken a step backward tonight. Thea hadn't known it. Olivia had soothed her and reminded her of how loved she was and always would be. By Olivia, by everyone, and especially by the father guarding her.

More tranquil now, Olivia's thoughts finally segued into what Eve had said about Matt. Was it possible Eve was right about that, too? *Was* Matt in love with her?

The idea thrilled her, but it also terrified her. Because she knew she was right, too. No matter how much they might care about each other, nothing could ever come of an attraction between them. It was hard enough living with Vivienne now. If Olivia and Matt should become involved in that way, there would be all-out war.

Vivienne would never sit still for another son of hers tying himself to Olivia.

So there was no point in thinking about Matt. If he *did* harbor feelings for her, he'd get over them. Especially if she discouraged him the way she had involuntarily done tonight by cutting off their conversation. She'd felt bad afterward, but now she realized the way she'd ended tonight's phone call might be the first step in distancing herself. Even so, she didn't want to hurt him. So what else could she do? She couldn't say anything, could she? No. Not unless he said something first.

You could date someone else.

Now that voice inside her was Eve again! Yes, Eve, she mentally answered, that would probably discourage him.

If Austin calls you, you should go out with him. And you should make a point of telling Matt.

Olivia closed her eyes. It saddened her to think of doing something so underhanded, but what other choice did she have?

On and on her thoughts went, replaying the phone conversation she'd had with Matt earlier, replaying everything she and Eve had discussed, going over and over the possibilities of how she could move forward with her life, perhaps build a new family with a daddy for Thea, yet somehow keep from causing Thea another loss, this time of her Britton grandparents—until finally Olivia fell into a fitful sleep.

Her dreams were as scrambled with emotions and people and events as her thoughts had been. Thea calling "Daddy!" Eve and Austin beckoning to her. Vivienne spewing hateful words. Her mother fainting. Erotic images of Matt. Those were the most vivid. Matt, kissing her, touching her, making love to her. The images of

Matt, so real and coming as they did just before dawn, caused her to awaken gasping, her heart pounding.

Later, after a long shower that soothed her and brought her back to reality, dressed and ready for the day, she stood at the kitchen counter in her blue scrubs waiting for her coffee to be ready and told herself that for her sake and for Thea's, she had to focus on going forward toward what was possible, even if it wasn't what she really wanted.

But it didn't really matter what *she* wanted, did it? Thea's welfare was far more important. So Olivia needed to suck it up and put ideas of Matt out of her mind for good. Because, unfortunately for her *and* for him, if he really did harbor romantic feelings toward her, her association with the Britton family had mostly brought her unhappiness and heartache and it didn't look as if that would ever change. It certainly wouldn't change if she and Matt became a couple.

Olivia was done with unhappiness. Done with heartache. She wanted something different in her life, something that promised peace and calm, happiness and security for both her and Thea.

And the only way to achieve that was to move on.

With someone other than a Britton.

"Say that again?" Matt couldn't believe he'd heard his father correctly.

"I said, your mother thinks we should petition family court for primary custody of Thea," his father repeated.

"I can't believe this. What possible grounds could you have?"

"Your mother feels this latest incident at the festival, added to the other incidents she's documented, will show that Olivia is an unfit mother."

"Other incidents? What other incidents?"

"Your mother's been keeping a list. Dates, times, circumstances, witnesses. She showed it to me, Matt. It's pretty incriminating."

"Dad, this is ridiculous. I can't believe you're in agreement with this."

"That list is bad, Matt. Your mother's right. Olivia doesn't seem responsible, just like your mother says."

Matt was appalled that his father could be taken in so easily. "This is the craziest thing I've ever heard. You know what? I'm coming over. I want to talk to both you and Mom together."

"Matt, I don't think that's a good—"

"I'm coming." He broke the connection.

Thirty minutes later, he was knocking at his parents' door. His father answered.

"Matt." He took Matt's arm, "I really wish you'd—"

Matt shook his father off. "Where's Mom?"

"She's in the sunroom, but—"

Ignoring his father, Matt strode straight back to the sunroom. He found his mother seated at the glass-topped table in front of the windows that looked out over the garden.

"Hello, Matthew," she said, looking up. She didn't smile.

"We were just about to eat lunch, son," his father said.

"And you were not invited," his mother said.

Before she'd finished speaking, Phoebe, their long-time cook, entered the room with a laden tray. "Oh, hello, Mr. Matt," she said. "I didn't know you were here. I'll get another plate."

"No need," his mother said in a clipped voice. "He's not staying."

"Oh, okay."

"Vivienne…" his father said.

She gave Matt's father one of her chilling looks, and whatever else he might have said died on his lips. He avoided Matt's gaze.

Matt sighed. He knew his mission was doomed to fail, but he had to at least try. He wouldn't be able to count on his father, though, that was obvious. He waited until Phoebe had unloaded the food: a bowl of shrimp salad, sliced tomatoes, French bread, butter and a pitcher of lemonade.

"That's all, Phoebe," his mother said, and Phoebe, who had hesitated, nodded and left the room, but not before giving Matt an apologetic glance.

Vivienne began filling her plate. "Sit down, Hugh."

Matt's father, whose role in their family had been determined long ago, shrugged and took his seat.

Matt, not about to allow his mother to cow him, too, pulled out one of the other chairs and joined them.

She turned toward him and narrowed her eyes. "I thought I made myself quite clear when I said you were not invited to stay."

"I have no intention of leaving until we talk about this latest craziness of yours."

"I beg your pardon?"

"I can't believe you are really going to try to take Thea away from her mother."

"Believe what you want."

"Mom, this is just wrong."

His mother put down her fork. "Matthew, I don't really care what you think. I will do what I know is best for my granddaughter. End of discussion."

"You're really willing to drag the Britton name through the mud? The *Marchand* name? Have everyone in Crandall Lake know your business?" Appealing to her family pride seemed the only avenue open to Matt, since it seemed to be highest on her list of priorities.

"*My* name won't be the one sullied, because I'm not the one who's unfit to raise Thea." So saying, she picked up her fork again and ate some of her shrimp salad.

Matt thought of ten things he could have said in rejoinder, but what was the use? Nothing would change his mother's mind, and his father didn't have the backbone to oppose her. "Fine. You're obviously determined to go down this path. But I won't be a party to it, and if you proceed, I won't help you."

"You would go against us?" his mother said in disbelief. "You would side against your own parents? Surely, even in your misguided state, you have to agree that Thea would be better off with us."

Matt shook his head. "No. I don't agree. Olivia is a good mother, and she doesn't deserve what you're doing to her." He pushed back his chair and stood. "She was Mark's *wife*, for God's sake. Think about what *he* would say if he were alive."

Her eyes narrowed. "I'm warning you, Matthew. Leave your brother out of this. And *you* stay out of it. Because if you don't, you will live to regret it."

With that last threat ringing in his ears, Matt turned and walked out of the room, leaving his parents to their lunch…and to each other.

But as he drove back to his office, he knew he had to warn Olivia. So after parking his car, and before heading inside, he took out his cell phone and called her work number.

"Registration and Admitting."

Matt didn't recognize the voice. "May I speak to Olivia Britton, please?"

"She's on her lunch break. Would you like to leave a message?"

"No, thanks. I'll call her cell."

Olivia answered on the second ring. "Hi, Matt."

"Hi. I called your work number first. I know you're at lunch. Can you talk?"

"Sure. I'm sitting outside, enjoying the beautiful day and eating my tuna sandwich."

"Well, I don't want to ruin your lunch hour for you, but something's come up that you need to know about."

"Oh?"

"Look, there's no way to sugarcoat this. My mother plans to petition family court for primary custody of Thea."

"What?"

The alarm in Olivia's voice was evident. Matt sighed. "I know. I was just as shocked as you are."

"On what grounds?"

"That you're an unfit mother."

"Oh, my God. You mean, because of Saturday?"

"Not just Saturday, apparently. My father says my mother's been keeping a list of incidents, with dates and times and witnesses."

"Incidents? What incidents?"

"I don't know. I haven't seen the list, and since I'm now persona non grata with my mother, I doubt I ever will." Actually, he was kicking himself for going on the attack with his mother before finding out exactly what *was* on that list.

"But, Matt—"

"I know, it's crazy. I went over there on my lunch break, tried to talk to her about it, but you know how she is. She just barreled right over me. Wouldn't listen. In fact, she threatened me."

"Threatened *you*? Why?"

"Because I sided with you. Told her I wouldn't go along with this."

"Oh, Matt, I don't want to cause any more trouble between you and your parents."

"You're not causing trouble. The trouble was there long before you came along."

"Is that true?"

"Yes, it's true. You remember the scandal involving Chet Parker? My mother bragged about bringing him down—she was actually proud of herself. And I've always thought she had a hand in Rosalie Harris's downfall. Someday I'll tell you all the gory details. But right now, we have more important things to worry about. I think we need to talk in person. Can you get your mother to watch Thea tonight? Maybe go out to dinner with me?"

"Um, yes, I'm sure I can, but..."

"But what?"

"Don't you think I need to do something to prepare? Like, immediately?"

"That's what I want to talk to you about."

"Oh, okay."

"How about if I pick you up around six thirty? Would that work?"

"Yes. That's perfect."

"All right, see you then."

"See you then," she echoed.

Matt sat in his car for long minutes after disconnecting the call. He knew he was on the precipice of something very dangerous, and that if he stepped off that cliff, he could never go back.

But if he didn't step off, if he allowed Olivia to fight

this on her own, he would never have any chance with her at all. There really wasn't any choice, was there?

He loved Olivia.

So he would do whatever it took to help her, no matter what else that path might cost him.

Because he knew, without any doubt at all, that without Olivia, his life would be meaningless anyway.

Chapter Five

Olivia still had ten minutes before she had to be back at her desk, so she used it to call Eve.

"Oh, my God," Eve said. "The woman is certifiable."

Olivia couldn't help laughing. Eve never did mince words. "We think so, but there are plenty of people who follow her lead."

"Tell you what, hon, as soon as we hang up, I'm going to call Austin. He's a top-notch attorney, and I know he'll represent you."

"Don't you think I should wait till I talk to Matt tonight?"

"No. I think you should line Austin up immediately. After all, we both know Matt can't represent you in this. He can be on your side privately and he can help from the sidelines, but he can't oppose his parents in court. I mean, think about it. If he fights her openly, your mother-in-law will just become more vindictive toward you."

Olivia did know that. It was one of the primary reasons she knew she could never have a romantic relationship with Matt, despite what Eve thought. She hesitated a moment, then said, "I would have to use some of Mark's insurance money to pay Austin, and I hate to do that. I wanted to keep it intact for Thea."

"Don't worry about the money, Liv. I'm paying his fee," Eve said. "And I don't want any argument about that, either."

"I can't let you do that."

"You're not letting me. I'm doing it, period."

"But—"

"No buts. Seriously. Adam has put so much money in my 'fun' account, as he calls it, I couldn't spend it all if I wanted to. Please let me do this for you."

Olivia's eyes filled with tears. "I love you, Eve."

"I love you, too. I'll let you know what Austin has to say."

"I don't want to talk about this while I'm at work. And I have to go back in a few minutes."

"I'll text you instead. And we can talk later tonight. After you've had dinner with Matt."

"All right."

They hung up then, and after Olivia tossed her trash, she headed back inside the hospital. She was filled with so many mixed emotions: disbelief and anger over Vivienne, gratefulness and relief over Matt's and Eve's support, and worry over the future.

She wondered what Mark would think if he knew what his mother was doing. He would be disgusted, she was sure. After all, he'd stood up to his mother when she tried to discourage him from marrying Olivia. Yes, Mark would be on her side. Of course, if Mark were alive, Vivienne would never even think of doing something like this.

Maybe not, but she'd have done her best to ruin your marriage.

Oh, God. What a mess everything was.

For the rest of the afternoon, Olivia couldn't give one hundred percent of her concentration to her job. How could she? At the back of her mind was always the thought of what could happen if Vivienne followed through on her threat. Even with Austin representing her, Olivia knew there was always the chance Vivienne could win, because the Britton family name carried tremendous influence in the county. In fact, Olivia had heard Vivienne had several judges in her pocket. Some of that was just gossip brought about by envy, but still… if there even a grain of truth in what was said, Olivia could be in for a rough ride.

I could lose. She could take Thea away from me!

Dear God. That couldn't happen. Eve was right. Olivia needed to be prepared with the best legal representation she could find. And aside from Matt, who was off-limits, Austin Crenshaw *was* the best. But what if Austin no longer wanted any part of this? Olivia wouldn't blame him if he didn't. After all, he had to live and work in Hays County, too, and Vivienne Britton could make a lot of trouble for him. *What will I do if he says no*?

She kept checking her phone, but Eve hadn't yet texted her. Olivia told herself that didn't mean a thing, that Eve had probably not been able to contact Austin yet, but still she worried.

Finally, at three thirty, a text came in.

Call Austin when you're free. He will take your case.
XXOO, Eve.

A giant wave of relief crashed through Olivia. Thank
God for Eve. What would Olivia do without her? Not
wanting to wait, Olivia told her supervisor she was taking a break, and she headed for a quiet corner of the
cafeteria where she placed a call to Austin's office. His
secretary put her right through.

"Olivia, hi," he said warmly. "Eve told me what's
happening with your in-laws."

"Yes, and she said you're willing to represent me."

"I'll be happy to represent you. But you know, it may
not come to that."

"What do you mean?"

"Well, your mother-in-law may change her mind.
Sometimes people threaten things, then back down
when their lawyers tell them what they're contemplat-
ing is not in their best interests. Or that they can't win."

Olivia wished. "You don't know Vivienne. She never
backs down."

"In that case, we'll be prepared. I'd like to meet with
you to go over everything. When would be convenient?"

"I'm off tomorrow."

"Great. Tomorrow afternoon works for me. Could
you come here to my office? Say about two?"

"I'll be there. And, Austin, thank you. I can't tell you
how grateful I am to have you in my corner."

"Like I said, happy to do it. I'd been meaning to call
you anyway." He hesitated a moment. "See if maybe I
could take you to dinner some night."

Olivia could hear the smile in his voice. He really
was so nice. Eve was right. Olivia could do a lot worse.
She resolutely pushed all thoughts of Matt out of her

mind. Matt had nothing to do with this. *Could* have nothing to do with it. She needed to remember that. She especially needed to remember it tonight. Because even if she were willing to take on the wrath of Vivienne Britton, she could never do that to Matt.

Olivia was still thinking about Matt and how to let him know, without ever saying anything directly, that there could never be anything more to their relationship than there was now, when he arrived to pick her up for dinner that evening.

"Right on time," she said as she answered the door.

When he smiled at her, her traitorous heart skittered. Why did he have to be so handsome? So sexy? And those eyes of his. An inky blue, they reminded her of the ocean at twilight. A girl could drown in their depths. He was everything a man should be. Not just sexy and good-looking, but strong, smart and kind. It still bewildered her that Matt had gone so long without marrying.

You could tell he was a Britton. There was an unmistakable resemblance between him and his siblings, although Matt was taller and darker than Mark had been. His hair was more chestnut, whereas her late husband's had been blond like Vivienne's.

Matt looked more like his father. So did Madeleine, the youngest of the family, who lived in Austin. Olivia was sure that's why Vivienne had favored Mark; he was the only one of her children who clearly belonged to her.

"You look very nice," Matt said now. His gaze swept her in admiration, taking in the black pencil skirt, the pretty pale blue silk sweater Eve had given Olivia for her birthday, and the black heels that fostered the illusion Olivia was taller than her actual five foot two.

"Thank you."

"Shall we go?"

"I'm ready."

"I thought we'd go to the inn."

Olivia frowned. "Are you sure you want to do that?" She knew he'd understand she was referring to the fact The Crandall Lake Inn was a favorite spot of his parents and their friends.

"I refuse to sneak around," he said firmly. "Unless you'd prefer to go somewhere else?"

"Actually, I would. Do you mind?"

"Of course not. What about Sam's Steakhouse?"

Olivia smiled. Sam's was a popular spot preferred by the younger set and was located nearer San Marcos than Crandall Lake. She doubted they'd see any of the Brittons' crowd there. "That sounds perfect."

Sam's wasn't as crowded on weekday nights as on the weekends, so they had no problem getting a table. And although all the window tables were occupied, Olivia actually preferred the quieter, more secluded corner table they were shown to.

Once they'd been seated, and their waiter had introduced himself, taken their drink order, and brought them their water and a basket of the warm rolls and herbed butter Sam's was known for, Matt said, "All day I've been thinking about my parents and what they're proposing to do."

"I know. Me, too. In fact—" But before she could finish, their waiter approached once more, this time bringing their drinks.

"What did you start to say before?" Matt asked when he left.

"Let's wait to talk until after we order our food."

"Okay."

It took a while to study the menu and decide what

they wanted, but finally their orders were placed, and Olivia could relax for a bit. "What I started to tell you before is that I've hired an attorney to represent me if your parents follow through on their custody threat."

Matt seemed taken aback. "I thought you'd wait till we talked. In fact, I have a recommendation for you."

"I *was* going to wait, but Eve arranged this for me. Her brother-in-law is taking my case. I'm sure you know him. Austin Crenshaw?"

"Of course I know Austin. He's a great lawyer. But he doesn't specialize in family law. I doubt he knows much about it. You need someone who not only knows case law, but also knows the judges and other lawyers who work in the field. You'll be at a disadvantage otherwise."

Olivia hadn't expected this. When Eve had suggested Austin, Olivia had been thrilled. On her own she never could have afforded a lawyer of Austin's caliber. But was Matt right? Was Austin a poor choice? Matt wouldn't say things unless he meant them, would he? Now what should she do? She'd already told Austin she wanted him.

"I'm looking out for your best interests, Olivia," Matt said quietly.

"I know you are. But Eve is, too." Olivia thought about telling him Eve was also paying Austin's fees, but admitting that would be embarrassing, so she said nothing.

"Even if you've already agreed to hire Austin, I think you should reconsider," Matt said. "Paul Temple is a friend of mine, and he's just about the best family law attorney in the county. If I asked him, I know he'd take your case and do a terrific job for you."

"If he's that good, maybe your parents have already signed him up."

"No, they've hired Jackson Moyer."

"How do you know that?"

"I asked around."

Jackson Moyer was famous in Hays County. He'd handled every high-profile case in recent memory. His name graced the pages of not just local newspapers, but the wire services and national network news shows. Olivia swallowed. Her earlier fear returned with terrifying clarity. "That's not good, is it?"

Matt started to answer, but just then, their waiter appeared with their food—the house special rib eye for Matt and the shrimp and scallops for Olivia. Matt waited until the waiter had left them alone again, before saying, "I knew my mother would want the best, so I wasn't surprised to find out they'd hired Moyer. But Paul Temple is just as good. Maybe not as showy, but totally on top of things. Moyer won't be able to run roughshod over him the way he does some attorneys."

When she didn't answer, he said, "Look, if you're worried about telling Crenshaw you've found someone else, I'll do it. I'll call him and talk to him. He'll understand."

"I appreciate your concern, Matt, I do. But I'm sure Austin will do a good job for me. After all, he represents his brother in all his dealings, and those are *huge* cases. Eve tells me no one likes tangling with him because he always wins."

"Yes, he's got a good reputation, and he's smart. But family law and family court are different animals, and it's not his specialty."

Olivia sighed. "I know, but I can't go back on my word."

"Olivia, this is too important for you to worry about

hurting someone's feelings. This is about Thea. She matters more than anything else, doesn't she?"

"Yes, of course, but—"

"Look, how about this? I'll ask Paul Temple if he'll assist. There's no law against you having a team of lawyers. I'm sure Jackson Moyer will have several assistants. He usually does."

"I don't know… I—" Cornered now, Olivia decided to tell Matt the truth. "I don't think I can afford more than one lawyer, Matt."

"Let *me* do this for you, Olivia."

"I can't. It…it wouldn't be right. And if your mother ever found out…"

"First of all, of course it's right. I'm Mark's brother. He would expect me to look out for you. And I'm Thea's godfather. And as far as my mother finding out, she won't. But even if she did, I really don't give a damn. I'm so tired of her and her machinations—"

"I appreciate the offer, Matt, but I can't accept. I—I won't come between you and your parents."

"I'm telling you, they won't know."

"This kind of thing always gets out, you know it does."

He sighed heavily, laying his fork down. "All right, Olivia. You win. But you're making a mistake, and I wish you'd reconsider."

Olivia knew he was disappointed in her. She wanted more than anything to reach across the table. To take his hand. To say she was sorry and admit that Eve was footing the bill for whatever this possible lawsuit would cost her. To add that his concern for her meant the world to her.

But she could say none of that.

If she did, he would view it as encouragement, and who knew where that would lead?

Remember, she told herself again, *you are not good for Matt. You will ruin whatever relationship he still maintains with his parents. And you will ruin his career in the process. In fact, you should not be here with him now. You absolutely* must *discourage him. No matter what it costs.*

"I wish none of this was happening," Matt said. "I still can't believe my parents are even thinking of doing this to you."

"I'm not really surprised," Olivia said. "I've always known your mother hates me."

"You took Mark away from her. She can't forgive you for that." He cut a piece of steak and ate it.

"Do you suppose she'd have felt that way about any girl he fell in love with?"

Matt shrugged. "The only girl she seems to approve of is Charlotte Chambers." He made a face. "Lately she's been pushing her on me."

"On *you*?" Olivia hoped the sudden stab of envy his words had caused didn't show in her face.

"Yeah. Ridiculous, I know."

"Not so ridiculous." Charlotte Chambers was everything Olivia was not. Tall, blonde, model beautiful, wealthy and a graduate of all the best schools. She had a pedigree a mile long and a name worthy of linkage with the Brittons.

"She doesn't interest me one iota," Matt said, eating more of his steak. "I find her bland and boring."

"Bland and boring!" Olivia very nearly started laughing. "How can you say that? She's perfect." She speared part of a scallop.

"That's the problem. She's so perfect, she feels she

doesn't have to say or do anything to be interesting."
He drank some of his wine. His eyes met hers over the
rim of the glass. "I prefer my women to be more down-
to-earth," he said, setting the glass down.

Olivia couldn't seem to look away, and for a long
moment, their gazes held. She knew suddenly that Eve
had been right. He *was* interested in her. Right now he
was telling her something he couldn't say out loud. She
only hoped she hadn't done or said anything to encourage him. Oh, Matt, she thought. Why did your name
have to be Britton?

After a few more seconds pregnant with unspoken
tension, Matt sighed and shook his head. "Tell Austin Crenshaw if he needs anything, anything at all, to
call me."

"Matt, I don't want you sticking your neck out for
me. You have a lot to lose, and if your mother—"

"You have more to lose than I do. And never mind.
You don't have to tell Austin anything. I'll call him
myself."

A tremor passed through Olivia as their gazes met
again. Right now she felt as though an avalanche was
on its way, and no matter what she did, she would not
be able to avoid its destruction.

Olivia dreamed of Matt again that night. The two of
them were somewhere warm, an island maybe. In her
dream, they were making love on a rumpled bed, with
the sound of the ocean somewhere near.

A warm breeze ruffled the sheer curtains, and
wooden shutters were open to the fragrance of tropi-
cal flowers. Birds sang, and somewhere in the distance
lilting guitars played irresistible melodies.

She moaned as his hands explored and caressed her.

The dream was so vivid, so real, that when they came together, she called out his name and woke up.

Heart pounding, she sat up in bed. Disappointment coursed through her. She was alone, the same way she'd been for more than four years now. The lovemaking hadn't been real. It could never be real. Not with Matt.

She looked at her bedside clock. It was 4:48 a.m. She would never get back to sleep, she knew she wouldn't. She had to get up at six o'clock anyway. Sighing, she tossed aside the light blanket, turned off the alarm and reached for her robe.

Downstairs, moving quietly so as not to awaken Thea, she fixed herself a cup of coffee and took it into the living room where she sat in her favorite chair and watched the sky slowly lighten. By the time she was ready to go upstairs and shower, she'd come to a decision.

Avalanche or no, she did not intend to allow anything to harm Thea, including her own foolish heart. She had to face it once and for all: loving Matt would come to no good.

In fact, it would destroy them all.

She couldn't allow that to happen. She *had* to begin pulling away from him. It was the only option she had.

"Oh, there you are. I've been looking for you."

Matt turned at the sound of Jenna Forrester's voice. As always, she looked impeccable and every bit the ideal ACDA—Assistant Criminal District Attorney—in her dark blue suit, tailored yellow blouse and sensible blue pumps, with her red hair swept back in a neat twist and secured by a gold clip. She was beautiful, smart and charming. He knew people felt she was the perfect partner for him. At one time, he'd thought so, too. Somehow, though, being perfect for him hadn't been enough. He'd needed passion, too, and it hadn't been there, no matter how much he might have wished it were.

"Hey, Jenna. What's up?" he said now.

"Wanted to give you this." She handed him a blue bound document.

He quickly scanned it: a motion to suppress evidence found during a search of the home of a defendant he was prosecuting. "How'd you happen to have this?"

She shrugged. "Guess they thought we were working together on the case."

Normally, they would have been. She had often been his second chair. But he'd been avoiding her since their breakup in August. "Thank you."

"You're welcome." She studied him for a moment. "You know, Matt, I'm not the vindictive sort."

"I know that."

"So stop avoiding me, then."

"Sorry. I thought it might be easier for everyone if—"

"Easier for you, you mean," she said, interrupting. Her smile was wry. "Seriously. There are no hard feelings."

He nodded, feeling like a bit of a heel. "I appreciate that."

"After all, why would there be? I mean, you can't help how you feel. Or don't feel. It's just my bad luck, right?"

Now there was an edge to her voice. Maybe she wasn't quite as understanding as she'd been pretending to be. "Why don't you just say it? I'm an idiot."

She chuckled. "You said it, not me."

"I'm sorry things have turned out this way, Jenna. You deserve better."

"Yes, I do. And I'm sorry, too. But I meant what I said. There are really no hard feelings."

"Thanks."

Their eyes met again, she gave him one last crooked smile, then waved goodbye and walked away.

Matt sighed again. Damn. Why was life so messy? Jenna really *was* perfect for him, unlike his mother's choice of Charlotte Chambers. Of course, Vivienne hadn't thought so, because Jenna wasn't in the same social circles. But none of that mattered, because neither woman was Olivia. And that was the problem, and always would be. Now that Olivia was in the same world and free to marry again, she was the only woman he wanted.

He hated that she'd hired Austin Crenshaw to represent her. He hadn't been able to stop thinking about it ever since she'd told him. Last night, as they'd said good-night at her front door, he'd been tempted to bring up the subject again, but he'd held off because he didn't want to upset her any more than she already was. Bad enough his mother bullied her. Olivia didn't need him bullying her, too.

But today, he decided he at least needed to reassure himself that Austin Crenshaw really would do a good job for her. So as he walked back to his office, he pulled out his cell and called Olivia. The call went directly to voice mail. She was probably still at work herself.

"Hey, Olivia, I was thinking. You said you were meeting with Austin Crenshaw tomorrow? I'd like to sit in at that meeting, because I'll know what questions to ask him, and you might not. Also, I'll be able to provide other information he might need. Call me back, okay?"

Because he was disciplined and because he took pride in his work, he managed to mostly put her and the custody suit out of his mind until he heard back from her.

She returned his call at six thirty. "I got your message."

He loved hearing her voice. "So it's okay if I go with you tomorrow?"

"I'm actually relieved you offered, because I probably *wouldn't* know the right questions to ask. My appointment is for two o'clock at Austin's office. Does that work for you?"

Matt would have to juggle some appointments, but that was okay. "No problem. Why don't I pick you up? We can go together."

She hesitated a few seconds. "Okay."

"I'll be there by one thirty."

He was smiling when they hung up. She needed him, whether she knew it yet or not. And he was determined to make sure that didn't change.

Still smiling, he decided since he'd be gone several hours tomorrow afternoon, he'd better stay late tonight and make sure everything for the Murphy trial was ready for next week's opening arguments.

Chapter Six

The smile had barely faded from Matt's face when there was a knock at his office door. Matt looked up as the door opened and his boss, Carter Davis, walked in.

"I'm glad I caught you," Davis said. "Thought you'd probably already gone for the day. Then I saw your lights on."

Matt smiled. He liked Carter. More important, he respected him. "I still have some stuff I need to do before I call it a night."

Carter lifted some files off the leather chair facing Matt's desk, put them on the floor and sat down. He studied Matt for a long moment.

Matt wondered what was up. Usually, when Carter wanted to see him, he summoned Matt to his office.

"Been wanting to talk to you about something," Carter finally said. His tone had turned solemn.

"Okay."

"You made any final decision about running for the House?"

Not sure where this was going, Matt decided to hedge. "I'm still mulling it over."

"But you're leaning toward doing it?"

Matt shrugged. "Truthfully? I'm not sure."

Carter nodded. "It's a big step."

"Yes."

The two men looked at each other. Carter hesitated, tented his hands, then said, "I don't like putting pressure on you, Matt, but I need you to make a decision, and soon. I've decided to retire the first of the year."

Even though Matt had expected something like this eventually, he was still a bit stunned. Carter had held the DA's position for twenty-eight years. He was practically a fixture in Hays County.

Seeing the expression on Matt's face, Carter smiled. "The governor will ask for my recommendation on a replacement to fill in until the next election. My pick would be you. And I know he would appoint you in the interim, but if you decide to go for the House and don't want to be DA, then I'll recommend someone else."

Matt let out a breath. Although he'd heard the rumors, he hadn't really expected Carter to retire this soon. That was one of the reasons he'd been receptive to the run for the House seat instead. *At least be honest with yourself. You were receptive because you were flattered. But now the flattery part has worn off, and reality has set in.*

"I know people have been speculating, so you must have thought about this possibility," Davis said.

"Yes."

Davis studied him a few seconds longer, then got up.

"I'll give you a week or so to think about it, but I'd like your answer fairly soon. Need to get that ball rolling."

In that instant, Matt knew what his answer was going to be. To hell with what his family wanted…or what his friends thought. This was his life, the only life he had. And everything he really wanted was right here, in Crandall Lake, not thousands of miles away.

But Matt wasn't the type of person to jump into anything. So he'd take a few days to think everything over thoroughly before giving Carter his answer.

But he couldn't help feeling excited about the way his career situation was shaping up. Now if only his personal life would keep pace, he would be one happy man.

Why had she agreed to let Matt go with her? Especially after what she'd decided this morning.

Yes, he'd be a help at the meeting, but she needed to begin standing on her own two feet, without relying on Matt so much. The more time she spent in his company, the harder it was to pretend they were only in-laws. She was afraid that one of these days she would give herself away by a word or a look. And then what?

Even if Eve had been right and Matt *did* care for her the way she'd begun to care for him, it was a go-nowhere situation. And no one knew that better than Olivia.

Why can't you stick to your convictions? You should have told him no today.

And yet, how could she? She didn't want to hurt him. And really, he'd been right. It *was* a wise thing to have him along with her today, because she didn't have a clue about what to ask Austin or whether he really *was* her best choice as a lawyer. Matt would be an invaluable help to her.

And wasn't Thea's welfare and keeping her daughter safe more important than anything else right now?

Of course, it was.

So all Olivia had to do was put on her big-girl panties, keep that thought uppermost, and she would be fine.

Matt left his office at one o'clock Wednesday and pulled into the driveway at Olivia's house shortly before one thirty. He'd barely rung her doorbell when the door opened. His heart squeezed at the sight of her. To him, she was more beautiful than any actress or model. Today she wore a dark blue dress with a simple string of pearls. The color emphasized the creaminess of her skin and the warmth of her eyes. It took all Matt's willpower to stop him from reaching for her. He wanted, more than anything, to pull her into his arms and kiss her. He wanted it so badly, he was sure she could feel the need emanating from him.

"Goodness," she said, smiling a little. "You look so official." Her gaze took in his dark pin-striped suit, white shirt and gleaming black shoes.

"My work uniform," he said, trying for a tone as casual as hers, even though the desire to touch her hadn't diminished. He managed to assuage that a bit by helping her into his car and breathing in her subtle scent.

"How's work going?" she asked once he was buckled in and had started the car. "You hardly ever talk about it."

"In the office, we refer to our work situation as OOU."

"OOU? What does that mean?"

He smiled. "Overworked, overwhelmed and understaffed."

She nodded. "Kind of sounds like the hospital."

"Just seems to be a fact of life most places nowadays."

"Can you afford to take this time off, then?"

"I have personal time coming to me."

She didn't answer, and Matt shot a glance at her. She was biting her lower lip. "Don't worry about it, Olivia. It's not a big deal." He considered telling her about Carter Davis's visit the previous evening, but decided this day was about her—her and Thea—not about him.

After a moment, Olivia smiled. "Thank you. I appreciate your doing this."

"I'd do anything for you…and Thea. You know that, don't you?"

"I… Yes. I do."

"So quit worrying." He knew she was always thinking about his mother and about not causing him trouble. One of these days, when the time was right, he would tell her everything, and do his best to make her understand that nothing she did or didn't do would make one bit of difference to the way his mother felt about him— *really* felt about him. It never had. And it never would.

It was a short drive to Austin Crenshaw's Crandall Lake office on the fourth floor of the First National Bank building on Main Street. They were silent as Matt pulled into the garage and parked. Five minutes later, they stood in Austin's office, ten minutes early for Olivia's appointment. The receptionist said she'd let Austin know they were there and disappeared into an inner sanctum.

A few minutes later, Austin walked into the waiting room. He seemed taken aback to see Matt sitting there, but he recovered quickly and gave Matt a smile, although he greeted Olivia first, taking her hand and saying, "It's good to see you again, Olivia. I'm only sorry about the reason."

"Thanks, Austin. I'm sorry, too."

Matt wished the man didn't seem so damned confident. He looked every inch the successful lawyer in a midnight blue suit that was obviously a designer label, paired with a dark red tie. Austin Crenshaw also had the good fortune to bear a marked resemblance to his famous brother, with the same dimpled smile and lanky grace. The only differences Matt could see were his short, professional haircut and the color of his eyes— hazel instead of Adam's much-written-about gray.

"I feel sure everything will be all right, though," Austin said. He was still holding Olivia's hand. Still smiling down into her eyes.

Matt had a childish urge to hit him. The feeling was so strong, he was afraid the emotion would show on his face.

Austin finally let go of Olivia's hand and turned to him. "I'm surprised to see you here, Matt," he said. "Since you're a member of the opposition camp."

"I don't happen to share my parents' feelings. I'm on Olivia's side all the way in this and will do whatever I have to do to help her."

"All right, then. Good. Let's go into my office, shall we?"

Austin took Olivia's arm, leaving Matt to follow them. Matt gritted his teeth. Austin's office was subtly elegant, with a jewel-toned Oriental carpet covering most of the hardwood floor, and classically designed furniture gracing its environs. Guiding Olivia to a rose-hued Queen Anne chair that was part of a grouping to one side of a shining mahogany desk, Austin took its mate next to her, leaving Matt to sit on the sofa facing them.

This put Matt at a disadvantage because he was seated lower than they were—part of the group, yet not part of it. His resentment grew, even as he understood Austin's strategy. The man was showing Olivia he was in charge, not Matt. In his shoes, Matt would have done the same.

Now, along with the desire to punch out Austin's lights, was a reluctant admiration. Clearly, Austin was a worthy adversary and certainly no fool. That he was interested in Olivia as more than a client was also evident because he hadn't taken his eyes off her more than a few seconds since they'd arrived, and his gaze was filled with warmth and undisguised admiration.

Although Matt was willing to concede the opening salvos to Austin, he knew it was time to take charge of this meeting and score his own points. "I'm sure you've done your research," he said. "So you know that my parents have hired Jackson Moyer."

Austin grimaced. "Yes, I know."

"I have to be honest with you, Austin. I don't think you're the best choice to represent Olivia. I think she needs an attorney more familiar with family court and the issues involved. Someone closer to Moyer's caliber. In fact, I recommended Paul Temple."

"I understand. But I can bring something to the case that Temple can't." Austin's gaze rested on Olivia. He smiled at her. "I care about Olivia personally and her case will be my top priority."

If Matt wasn't convinced before that Austin was thinking of Olivia as far more than a client, he was convinced of it now. And he also knew if he wanted a prayer of success with her himself, he didn't have long to make his move. Although she might shoot him down, wasn't that better than never taking a chance at all?

For the next hour and a half, both he and Olivia gave Austin all the information he asked for, plus some he hadn't. And Matt promised he would try to find out exactly what kind of "evidence" his mother had compiled against Olivia.

"That should be a part of discovery," Austin said.

Matt shrugged. "You'd think, wouldn't you? But knowing Moyer, I'm certain he'll figure out a way to keep it under wraps until we're actually in court. He likes the big reveal, the drama inherent in surprising his opponents." His glance met Olivia's, and he saw the worry in her eyes. "I'll try to get the information, though."

Olivia made a face. "I don't know, Matt. Your mother knows you don't agree with her. I doubt she'll tell you anything. And you'll just make things worse between the two of you."

"I agree she probably won't tell me, but my father might."

"I hate this," Olivia said. "I don't want to cause any more trouble for you."

"You're not causing it. My mother's responsible for that."

"But you're their son…"

"And you're their son's widow. And the mother of his child."

"Your brother-in-law's right, you know," Austin interjected.

Matt felt a moment of irritation. He didn't need Austin's help. Nor did he need him pointing out their relationship. He almost said something, but the moment passed. It would be stupid of him to argue with Austin or try to make his job harder. They both wanted the same thing. To help Olivia win her case and keep her daughter. In this, at least, they were in perfect accord.

"I'll file our response to the complaint tomorrow," Austin said as both Olivia and Matt stood. "And I'll call you when I have anything to report." Once again, he reached for her hand, keeping it in his much longer than necessary. "Actually, I'll call you tomorrow, regardless."

Matt's jaw clenched.

"Thank you. I'm feeling more hopeful now that we've all talked," Olivia said. She withdrew her hand and smiled at him.

Austin seemed reluctant to turn to Matt. They shook hands, and they all said their goodbyes, with Austin re-iterating he would call Olivia. As Olivia and Matt rode the elevator down to the parking level, they were both silent, and he wondered what she was thinking about. Was she worried about the upcoming custody battle? Or was she thinking about Austin and his attention to her?

Matt wasn't sure. In fact, the only thing he was sure about was that he had no time to lose. Today, for the first time, he could feel her slipping away from him, and he couldn't let that happen.

He had to think of ways to spend more time with her. To maybe bring their situation to a head without seeming to pressure her.

"So did you mean what you said in there? You do feel more hopeful now that Austin's on the case?"

"Yes, I do. What about you?"

They had reached Matt's car by now, and he un-locked it and helped her in before answering.

"I'm still not convinced he's going to do as good a job as Paul Temple would do," Matt said once they were on their way. "One thing was clear today, though."

"What?"

"He likes you. In fact, I'd say he likes you a lot. So I'm sure he'll do his best to impress you." He glanced over at her to see her reaction.

Just from her body language and her hesitation in answering, he knew she was probably uncomfortable. Maybe even blushing. Olivia blushed easily. In fact, most of the time she wore her emotions for all to see. That was another thing he loved about her. There was never any subterfuge with Olivia. She was genuine through and through.

"He was just being nice, that's all," she finally said.

"You know," Matt replied carefully, "I don't blame him for being interested. Why wouldn't he be? You're a beautiful woman. And Mark's been gone a long time."

"First of all, I'm not beautiful. And second, yes, Mark *has* been gone a long time, but I can't think about anything like that right now, Matt. I have to concentrate all my energy on this lawsuit."

"You *are* beautiful, Olivia. I've always thought so."

"I…" She stopped, looked out the window. "Can we please change the subject? You're…making me uncomfortable."

"Sorry. I didn't mean to."

"I know. It's just that… I'm not ready for a discussion about dating."

He knew he'd pushed as far as he could right then. "Fair enough. New subject. Want to grab an early bite to eat before I take you home?" He had lightened his tone, but he felt encouraged, because he sensed something in the way she had reacted to him. Something that told him maybe, just maybe, he had a chance.

"Thank you, but Thea and I are having dinner at my

mom's. She's making one of our favorites—*haluski*." She pronounced it ha-loosh-key.

"Haluski?" He'd never heard of it.

"It's an ethnic dish, basically noodles and cabbage, fried with lots of onions and butter. I made it for Mark a couple of times. He loved it."

"Maybe I should invite myself to dinner," Matt said lightly.

Olivia looked at him. "Seriously?"

"Seriously." He grinned. "Single guys don't get many home-cooked meals."

Once again, she hesitated before answering. "Well, I know Thea will be thrilled if you stay to dinner."

"Only Thea?"

Suddenly Olivia laughed. "My mother will be thrilled, too. She likes you."

"What about you?"

"Are you digging for a compliment?"

"Everyone likes compliments."

"Okay. I'm glad you want to have dinner with us. There. Are you satisfied?"

Now that the tone of their conversation had changed, he decided to make one more attempt to burrow through her defenses. "I was hoping you'd say you liked me, too."

He could feel her looking at him, but he kept his eyes on the road.

After a long moment passed, she finally said, "Of course I like you, Matt. You're part of the family."

Because they were now approaching her mother's house, he let the comment go without answering. Because she was sending mixed signals, whether she knew it or not.

"Think it's okay for me to park in the driveway?" he asked a few seconds later.

"Sure."

Olivia didn't knock first or ring the doorbell. She simply opened the door and walked in, beckoning him to follow. "Mom," she called out, "we've got company for dinner."

Norma Dubrovnik, looking like an older version of her daughter, emerged into the hallway. She was flushed, wearing an apron, and it was obvious she'd been cooking. She smiled when she saw Matt. "Oh, hi, Matt. It's good to see you."

He smiled back. He liked her. She was just the kind of woman he wished his mother was. "Hi, Mrs. D. I hope you don't mind, but I invited myself to dinner."

"I don't mind at all. I always make enough for an army."

Just then, Thea came running out from behind her grandmother. "Unca Matt!" she exclaimed as they entered the house. "I'm getting a kitten!" Her smile lit her entire face.

"You are?" he said, scooping her up and twirling her around.

She giggled. "Yes!

"You're a lucky girl," Matt said, nuzzling Thea's cheek.

"I know!" Thea said, squirming out of his arms and running down the hall where she was out of earshot.

"She's talked of nothing else since I told her we'd go soon," Olivia said. She frowned. "But if we get a kitten, I don't know what we're gonna do on the days Thea has to go to day care. She won't want to leave the kitten at home."

"Maybe I could take a leave of absence from work," Norma said. "Then you could bring them both here instead of taking her to day care, especially while all this other mess is going on." She'd dropped her voice, although Thea had disappeared into the kitchen again.

Olivia's mouth dropped open. "A leave of absence? What will Dr. Ross say? Who will do your job? Thea is my responsibility, not yours."

"Dr. Ross can get a temp the way he does when I'm on vacation. I know if I talked to him he'd understand," Norma said.

"No, I don't want you to do that. Besides, Mom, you do enough as it is, picking her up from day care and keeping her when I work the afternoon shift."

"What do you think, Matt?" Olivia's mother said, turning to him. "Wouldn't Olivia's case be stronger if Thea wasn't in day care at all anymore?"

Matt hated to disagree with Olivia, but he thought her mother was right. He nodded reluctantly. "Your mom has a point, Olivia."

Olivia sighed. "I'll think about it. Maybe *I'm* the one who needs to quit working."

By now, they'd moved into the kitchen, and Matt, lured by the good smells wafting from the big cast-iron skillet on the stove, walked over and peered at its contents. "Looks great," he said. "Smells great, too." He was a sucker for any kind of pasta.

"Wait'll you taste it," Olivia said.

"I made sausage, too," her mother said.

"Better and better," Matt said.

"Maybe, since Matt's here, we should eat in the dining room," Norma said.

"Mom, don't fuss. Matt doesn't care," Olivia said.

"I'd rather eat in the kitchen," he said. "It's cozier."

Norma was still making noises about the dining room as Olivia got Thea settled into a booster chair, but finally the food was on the table and the four of them had taken their seats. Matt grinned when he saw the size of the serving bowl containing the cabbage and noodles.

"You weren't kidding about feeding an army, were you?" he teased Olivia's mother.

She laughed and brushed her hair back from her forehead. "It's ingrained. In our house, growing up, putting a lot of food on the table showed you cared about your family."

"Actually," Olivia interjected, "it showed you could afford to *feed* your family. Right, Ma?"

Norma gave her a sheepish smile. "Yes, that's true."

Matt couldn't help but think about how different his own home had been. He couldn't ever remember a homey scene like this one. All Britton meals had been served in the dining room, and certain dress and behavior were de rigueur.

Just then, Thea hit the table with her spoon. "I'm hungry!" she announced.

They all laughed, and Olivia took her plate and filled it with the noodles. Then she cut up a piece of sausage and transferred half of it to Thea's plate, as well. Thea immediately dug in as the rest of them served themselves.

Matt couldn't remember anything tasting so good. He knew part of his enjoyment had to do with the company he was with, but the food really was great. So was the talk and laughter and genuine love among them. Matt had always known something was missing from his own family, and now he fully understood what it was: the knowledge that these people cared for him more than any other people in the world.

His heart felt full as he looked around the table. Right now, at this moment, he was home.

And home was where he wanted to stay.

Chapter Seven

Olivia knew what she was doing and feeling was crazy but having Matt there with them made her happier than she'd been in a long, long time. It just felt so right, so natural. And she knew she wasn't alone in feeling this way. She could see how much her mother liked him. And, of course, Thea loved him.

And I love him. That's the problem. That's why it's so impossible to stick to any decision that has to do with easing him out of my life.

She had been so uncomfortable in the car today when Matt said those things about Austin. And about her. She'd wanted to say there was only one man who interested her in that way, and that man wasn't Austin. But how could she?

If only things were different.

If only Matt wasn't a Britton.

If only Vivienne was a normal mother-in-law, someone who loved her and wanted her to be happy.

Much of Olivia's happiness faded. Vivienne *wasn't* normal. And Olivia wasn't free to love Matt. To even *hint* at how she felt. Her love would cost him his family. And possibly his career.

Don't ever forget that.

Perhaps her eyes or her expression betrayed her thoughts, because Matt's eyes met hers and he frowned. Olivia made a determined effort to smile and pretend everything was just as good as it had been moments before, but she was afraid she hadn't succeeded, because his eyes remained curious and his own smile seemed strained.

Thank goodness for her mother. Norma stood and said, "Is everyone ready for dessert?"

"Ice cream!" Thea shouted.

"Not ice cream," Norma said. *"Kolache."*

"Kolache!" Now Thea laughed happily. *"Kolache and* ice cream!"

"She's got you there, Mom," Olivia said. Turning to Matt, she added, "You'll love my mother's *kolache*, Matt. She makes one kind with walnuts. And another kind with apricots. They're both wonderful."

"And sometimes poppy seed," Norma said.

He grinned, the strain gone. "I can't wait."

Olivia got up and began clearing the table. Surprising her, Matt stood, too, and helped.

"Sit, sit," Norma said. "Our guests don't do kitchen duty."

"This guest does. I invited myself, remember?" He turned to Thea. "Let's get you cleaned up a bit, princess."

"You're silly. I'm not a princess." But she allowed him to wipe her face and hands.

"You're *my* princess," he said, ruffling her hair.

Thea giggled.

Olivia's heart squeezed at his tender words. He would make a wonderful father because it was easy to see he loved Thea. In fact, he'd shown time and again that he really liked kids, not just Thea. Some men only pretended to, but with Matt it was genuine, and kids responded accordingly. He even helped coach a Little League baseball team and had once said he couldn't wait until he had a son of his own to coach. Yes, he'd make a terrific father.

If only… But she cut the thought off. "Time for dessert," she said brightly instead.

Minutes later they were all settled around the table again. The adults had fresh coffee with their slices of *kolache*, and Thea happily ate Blue Bell Homemade Vanilla ice cream to go along with hers.

"This is the best *kolache* I've ever had," Matt declared.

"It's different than what you usually find in Czech communities," Norma said, "but it's the way my grandmother made it."

She was referring to the fact she baked long jelly-roll-like pastries, then sliced individual servings. Most Czech bakers made stand-alone fruit *kolaches*, with a well in the middle containing fruit or jam.

"Well, they're wonderful," Matt said.

Olivia made a determined effort not to let her thoughts stray into dismal territory again, and for the most part, she felt she was successful. After they'd finished their dessert, Olivia and Matt cleaned up the kitchen. He even allowed Olivia to give him an apron.

"I'm not going to be responsible for you ruining that suit," she said, knowing it was expensive.

"Slave driver." But he was laughing.

She laughed, too, especially when she saw how cute he looked in the frilly apron. "That suits you." She pretended to reach for her phone. "I think I need a picture. To post on Facebook."

"I'll kill you if you take one." He wielded a wooden spoon as if it were a weapon.

Still laughing, she mock-ducked.

After more silly banter, the kitchen was clean and Norma suggested they go into the living room "where it's more comfortable."

They passed another pleasant hour talking and watching Thea play with the Lego set Norma kept in a toy box for her beloved granddaughter. But at seven o'clock, Olivia reluctantly said she thought it was time to go. No matter how much she loved this part of the day, it couldn't last forever. "Put the Lego away, sweetie," she said to Thea.

"I don't want to," Thea said, pouting.

"Thea," Olivia said.

Thea's lower lip protruded.

"I mean it."

With a long-suffering sigh, Thea began to very slowly put each Lego piece in the toy box.

Olivia considered saying something about speeding it up, but didn't. It was enough that Thea was obeying.

"Need some help with that, princess?" Matt said, getting down on the floor with her.

"Matt... "

He looked up, and when his eyes met hers, the rest of what Olivia was going to say died on her lips. There was something undeniable in his eyes, something Olivia knew she was going to have to deal with. The only question was, how? Because here...and now...she knew it wasn't going to be easy to walk away from him, no matter how much she knew it would be the right thing to do.

Why does he have to be so wonderful? And why am I so attracted to the absolute wrong man?

Heart pounding, she looked away and began gathering her things.

Finally they were ready to leave.

At the door, when Norma hugged Olivia goodbye, she whispered, "He would make Thea a wonderful father."

"Mom!" Olivia whispered back. What if Matt had heard her?

But he hadn't. He'd instead picked up Thea and was allowing her to sit piggyback, which she loved to do. She was giggling and he was pretending to be a horse, complete with neighing sounds as he transported her outside to the car.

All the way home—which was only minutes away—Olivia couldn't get her mother's comment out of her mind. Hadn't she thought the same thing earlier? That Matt *would* make a wonderful father? And he'd probably make an even more wonderful husband.

And lover.

That thought made her breath catch, almost as if she'd said it out loud. She glanced over at Matt, but he wasn't looking at her. Thank God. Even though she'd not voiced that thought aloud, her eyes might have betrayed her.

When they reached her house, she turned to say goodbye to him at the door, but he said, "I'll come in. Help you get Thea ready for bed."

"You don't have to do that, Matt. I know you have things to—"

"I want to."

What could she say? *I don't want you to.* That would be a lie because she did want him to. The fact was, she wanted even more. She wanted, after they'd gotten Thea ready for bed and settled her into her room, to take Matt's hand and lead him into the master bedroom. She wanted him to stay the night. She wanted him to undress her and make slow love to her, not once, but several times.

She remembered that old song from the oldies station her mother used to listen to—the one about slow hands.

She swallowed.

Just thinking about what she wanted made her stomach feel hollow.

It had been so long. So very long. She could hardly remember what it had been like to be held, to be loved, and touched, and cherished. She and Mark had been too young, really. Their lovemaking had been fast and impatient, the way young lovers are. Mark had never had the chance to grow with her.

She was so lonely.

Her loneliness hadn't been so bad when Eve was living there, when they'd been in the same boat, but now Eve had found love again. A wonderful, passionate, grown-up love. All you had to do was look at her to see how happy she was. How fulfilled.

I want that, too. I deserve that, don't I?

Why was she torturing herself? She knew what she wanted couldn't happen. That's all her neighbors would need. To see Matt's car in her driveway all night long. The entire gossip network of Crandall Lake would be on overtime tomorrow!

And Vivienne.

She would go ballistic.

Olivia actually shuddered, thinking of it.

"What's the matter?" Matt said. By now they'd settled Thea into her bath and were sitting watching her. "Are you cold?"

Olivia shook her head.

"You sure?"

Olivia tried hard to make her smile genuine. "Yes, I'm sure." She could feel his eyes on her as she looked away.

After Thea's bath was finished, Olivia dressed her in her pj's and got ready to read her a story. She hoped Thea wouldn't ask for the daddy story tonight, because she wasn't sure she could handle that kind of emotion right now. Not in front of Matt.

But Thea surprised her, saying in her stubborn voice, "I want Unca Matt to read to me, Mommy."

Olivia looked at Matt, who stood in the doorway.

He smiled. "I'd love to."

Olivia sat in the rocking chair in the corner while Matt sat next to Thea on her bed and read her *Pigtastic!*, one of her favorite stories. Olivia loved looking at him, loved seeing the way Thea responded. It was clear he was enjoying himself, that none of what he was doing was pretense. No one was that good an actor. With every moment that passed, Olivia realized anew what she would have if she could have Matt.

By the time he'd finished, Thea's eyes were closing. It had been a long, full day, and she was obviously tired.

Olivia got up and went over to the bed. "Say goodnight to Uncle Matt, honey."

"'Nite, Unca Matt."

"Good night, sweetheart." He bent over and kissed Thea's cheek.

Then Olivia kissed her daughter, too, saying, "Sweet dreams, pumpkin. I love you."

"I love you, too, Mommy."

Olivia turned off the carousel lamp, leaving only the night-light on, and she and Matt where almost out of the room when Thea said, "Unca Matt?"

He stopped, turning to look back at Thea. "Yes, sweetheart?"

"I wish you were my daddy."

Olivia's startled eyes met his. For a long moment, their gazes held. Then Matt, still looking at Olivia, said, "I wish that too, sweetheart."

Thea's words and Matt's answer thundered in Olivia's mind as they left Thea's room and walked to the front of the house. Olivia knew she should say something, but she couldn't think of anything. She could barely look at Matt, let alone make conversation.

"I guess I'd better go," he said.

"Yes," she murmured.

When they reached the door, he turned to her. "Liv."

She finally raised her eyes. Her heart felt unsteady.

"I meant what I said. I do wish I was Thea's father. Just as I wish you were…mine."

Then, shocking her, he drew her into his arms, lowered his head and captured her mouth in a kiss that sent lightning bolts all the way to her toes.

Knowing he'd stunned her, Matt almost said he was sorry. But he wasn't sorry. And Olivia had responded to his kiss, opening her mouth and allowing him in for long seconds before pushing him away. That had to mean something.

"Matt, we…we can't do this." Her troubled eyes met his as she backed away from him.

He reached for her, taking her hand. "Why not?"

"You know why not."

"What I know is, I'm tired of pretending to just be your brother-in-law when I'd like to be so much more. And I think you *want* me to be more."

"I just… I don't see how you *can* be more. You know how your mother feels about me. She'd go crazy if she thought there was anything between us."

"That would be *her* problem, wouldn't it?"

"It would also be our problem."

"Not mine. I don't care what she thinks. Think about it, Olivia. She's going to go crazy when I testify as a character witness for you, so what's the difference?"

"You're planning to be a *character* witness for me?"

"Of course I am."

"You can't do that, Matt."

"I can, and I will."

"But—"

"No buts. I'm doing it. You and Thea are more important to me than anyone else in the world, and I don't care who knows it."

Olivia sighed shakily. "Knowing that means a lot to me, Matt. But are you sure? Your mother won't sit still for this."

Matt shrugged. "Let her do her worst."

"I…" Another shaky sigh. "Matt, you have to give me some time. This is a lot to process."

"I know it is. I don't expect you to make me any promises. I just wanted you to know how I feel." He didn't add that he'd wanted to make sure he staked his claim before Austin Crenshaw started working on her.

Their eyes met again, and he could see all the confusion and doubt and fear raging through her. At that moment, he could have cheerfully strangled his mother. This mess was all her doing. If Vivienne was a normal person, with normal feelings, she would want her son's widow to find happiness again. She would *encourage* her. And if that happiness was with her other son, she would be ecstatic. But Vivienne wasn't normal. And, for some reason Matt had been trying to figure out all his life, she didn't have the same feelings for him as she'd had for Mark.

"Just tell me one thing," he said.

"What?" Olivia said softly.

"Do I have a chance?"

She closed her eyes. "Oh, Matt…"

"Do I?"

"I—I do care for you. In fact, I more than care for you, but I…" Her face twisted. "I don't want a life filled with tension and estrangement from family. It was hard enough with Mark…before Thea. I just can't go through all of that again. And it would be worse now. I know it would. If…*when*…I win this custody case, I want something different. I—may have to move away to get it. I don't want to do that, but if that's what it takes for a peaceful life, that's what I'll do."

His heart sank. He could see the truth of what she was saying in her eyes. And he felt it in his bones. "Please don't make any decisions yet. Just wait. Okay? Will you promise me that? Anything can happen."

She slowly nodded. "I promise I'll wait. I won't decide anything for sure yet. I need time. And as I said before, if your mother follows through on filing for custody of Thea, I'll need to focus every bit of my energy on defeating her."

"And I'll do everything in my power to help you do that."

"Thank you," she whispered. Then, as if to take the sting out of what she'd said earlier, she rested her head against his chest and hugged him. "Good night, Matt. And thank you for everything."

He allowed himself to hold her for a long moment, then kissed the top of her head, inhaling its clean, fresh fragrance, and whispered, "I love you," and left.

As Matt walked out to his car, his thoughts were in turmoil. But one thing he was sure of. He might lose, but that didn't mean he wouldn't give everything he had into fighting for Olivia.

Even if it meant he would have to walk away from everything here and begin again somewhere new.

Olivia leaned against the door after Matt left. His kiss, and everything he'd said, had shaken her to her core. She'd wanted to tell him that being with him today had meant everything to her, that having him as her husband and as Thea's father would be the answer to all her prayers.

But that couldn't happen.

Because no matter how she felt, she'd meant what she told him. She did want something different. She wanted a close, warm, loving relationship with both her family and a potential husband's family. And that would never happen with Matt and the Brittons. Vivienne would never accept her. Even if she mounted a fight to gain custody of Thea and lost, Vivienne would continue trying to undermine Olivia. She would continue fighting her and finding fault with her and working to make her life miserable.

But Olivia had to be strong. She could no longer allow her mother-in-law to do these things. For the longest time, Olivia had felt she had to do everything in her power to keep communication with Vivienne as pleasant as possible, no matter what the older woman said or did. But this probable suit against her, Vivienne's threat to wrest Thea away, had proven to Olivia that nothing would ever change. And if she allowed Vivienne to continue in this spiteful vein, it would impact Thea's life in ways Olivia couldn't...*wouldn't* tolerate.

So for everyone's good, but most especially Thea's, Olivia would need to start a new life...probably somewhere far away from Crandall Lake and everything Britton.

Olivia was still turning all these thoughts over in her mind thirty minutes later after changing into her pajamas and pouring herself a glass of wine, with the intention of putting her feet up and watching the latest recorded episode of *The Good Wife*, one of her guilty pleasures, when her cell rang.

Olivia smiled; it was Eve.

"I wondered how your meeting with Austin turned out," Eve said. "But I gave up on you calling me, so I decided I'd call you."

"It's been a long day," Olivia said. She sank into her favorite chair and put her bare feet on the matching ottoman.

"Well? How'd it go?"

Olivia gave her an abbreviated version of the meeting.

"Has Matt come around to agreeing Austin's a good choice for you?" Eve asked.

"Sort of." Olivia hesitated, then decided it would be good to have Eve's opinion of everything that happened after the meeting. "He said it was clear Austin would work hard for me because Austin likes me."

"Oh, really? Did he mean *likes* you as in wants to date you?"

"Yes."

"And what did you say?"

"I said I wasn't sure I was ready for that and that I needed to put all my energy into this court case."

"Is that what you're going to tell Austin if he asks you out?"

"I don't know." Maybe it would be best to go out with Austin if he asked her. Maybe that would be the only way to make Matt forget about her. "Um, something else happened today. Later on."

"I'm all ears."

"Matt invited himself to dinner at Mom's. And then afterward, he came in to help put Thea to bed. And after he kissed her good-night, she said she wished he was her daddy."

"Oh, Liv."

"I know."

"What did you say?"

"I was too rattled to say anything. But then Matt was leaving to go home, and he said he wished the same thing. And that he wished I was his, too. Then he…he kissed me."

"Wow."

"Yeah."

"Did you kiss him back?"

"I couldn't help myself. But then I pushed him away."

"See? I *told* you he felt that way about you."

"I know you did." Olivia sighed.

"So what happened then? After you pushed him away?"

Olivia repeated the rest of the conversation between her and Matt. "I'd give anything if things were different, Eve. But they aren't. And I meant what I said. I don't want a repeat of my marriage to Mark."

"I totally understand. And you deserve that. Frankly,

I don't think a relationship with Matt could survive the continuous onslaught of viciousness Vivienne would subject you to. Not to mention she could totally ruin Matt's career."

"I know."

Eve was silent for a few seconds. Then, thoughtfully, she said, "You know, Liv, you should seriously think about moving out here. Adam was just saying today that he desperately needs to hire a secretary/assistant to take care of things here, not just for his career, but for our personal lives, too, which would mean basing someone here in the house, but he didn't know how I'd feel about having a stranger among us. But if it was *you*…oh, my goodness, that'd be perfect. And you'd be perfect for the job. Oh, Liv, think about it, will you? I know you'd have to wait till the custody hearing is over, but after that… it's the ideal solution. There's even a separate place you could live and have your privacy. We have a guesthouse adjacent to the pool. It has two bedrooms and its own kitchen! The previous owner's mother lived there, so it's entirely self-sufficient. And we have tons of room in the house. There are six bedrooms! Your mom, my mom, Stella, they could all come to stay, whenever they wanted to. It would be wonderful. I would love it. The kids would love it!"

Later, as Olivia settled into bed, she couldn't stop thinking about Eve's suggestion. Everything in her felt sick at the thought of leaving Crandall Lake and Matt. But in her heart of hearts, she knew she was close to a place where she could no longer handle Vivienne and her vindictiveness.

Nor did she want Thea exposed to it, grandmother or no grandmother.

Maybe moving away was the only choice left.

Chapter Eight

Matt waited until Monday morning to call Carter Davis's office. "Is he free to see me for a few minutes?" he asked Mary, Carter's longtime secretary, now officially called his admin.

"Let me check." A few seconds later, she said, "He said to tell you he's got twenty minutes before he has to leave for an appointment in Austin."

Two minutes later, Matt accepted a cup of coffee from Mary and settled into one of the chairs in front of Carter's desk. "I've come to a decision," he said.

"Okay." Carter put down the pen he'd been using to sign some documents.

"I'm not going to run for the House seat. I'll notify my biggest supporters today."

Carter seemed surprised. "You're sure about this?"

"Very sure."

"I have to admit, I wasn't certain you'd go this way. But I'm glad. I think you're the best person for the job.

It'll make stepping down a lot easier for me, knowing I'm leaving everything in your hands."

"Well," Matt said, "I still have to win an election next year."

"No doubt in my mind that you will."

"Nothing's a sure thing when voters are involved."

"You'll have me in your camp." Carter stood, extended his hand, then clapped Matt on the back as he walked him out.

Heading back to his own office after leaving Carter's, Matt felt a twinge of guilt. He knew he should have been completely open with Carter and told him there was a possibility he would not be able to follow through on running for district attorney in the next election, that there was a chance—a slim one, but still a chance— that he might actually have to move to another state, and why. But he hadn't said anything because he hoped matters would never come to that. And he'd known if he confessed this possibility to his boss, no matter how slim, Carter would not have felt comfortable recommending him to the governor.

Damn his mother. Why couldn't she be a normal mother, someone who was proud of him and wanted him to be happy?

He tried to wipe the entire problem out of his mind as he reentered his office and began to deal with the day's schedule, and he was nearly successful until his phone rang an hour later and the caller turned out to be his mother's favorite candidate for a daughter-in-law, Charlotte Chambers.

"I haven't seen much of you lately," she said, "and decided to take matters into my own hands and give you a call."

"I've been buried in work," he said. "I'm buried now." Maybe she'd take the hint.

"I figured as much, especially since you're getting your ducks in a row for your campaign for the House seat."

"Yes, lots of things going on," he answered smoothly. He wasn't ready to advertise the fact he didn't intend to run for the House seat. Not until he'd had a chance to talk to the people who had been supporting him. He owed it to them not to say anything to anyone else before notifying them. He especially didn't want Charlotte to even suspect. Knowing her, the first person she'd call would be his mother.

"Surely you can take a break now and then," Charlotte said in a flirty voice.

He made a noncommittal sound. Good thing she couldn't see his expression.

"Anyway, that's why I'm calling," Charlotte continued. "I was hoping to persuade you to accompany me to the Harvest Ball next week." The Harvest Ball was one of the biggest charity events of the year, with the proceeds going to the new women's health center that would serve the entire county.

"Thanks, Charlotte, but I can't. I have another commitment."

"Oh, darn. I'm disappointed. It would have been good for your campaign to be seen there."

"I'm sure you're right. But it can't be helped." He knew she wanted to know what his commitment was, but he refused to fall into the trap of trying to explain. Especially since there was no commitment. But mostly because he didn't owe her an explanation.

"I'm sorry for another reason," she said, her voice

softening. "I miss you. I've barely seen you in the last few months."

"That's what happens when you're trying to raise money for a campaign as well as holding down a job that requires sixty- and seventy-hour weeks. Your friends get neglected."

She didn't say anything for a long moment. When she did, her voice turned coy. "All right. You get a pass this time. But I think you owe this friend a rain check, don't you? In fact, I know just how you can make it up to me."

Matt mentally thought a bad word.

"My sorority is having a casino night the Friday after Halloween. It's loads of fun and all the profits will be donated to the children's museum. You can be my date that night."

"I can't promise anything, Charlotte. I'll check on some things and get back to you. I may be out of town that weekend."

"Now, Matt, I'm not going to listen to any more excuses. You work far too hard."

What was he going to have to do? Come right out and tell her he was not interested? He couldn't help comparing her to Olivia. Hell, there *was* no comparison. Olivia was a beautiful, warmhearted, kind woman and Charlotte was all flash, no substance. However, she seemed to have the hide of an elephant. Hints didn't make a dent. In fact, in this regard, she bore a decided similarity to his mother. With a mental sigh, he knew he could no longer postpone the inevitable.

"Look, Charlotte," he said, keeping his voice as pleasant as he could manage, "we're both adults and I know you're the kind of person who would prefer honesty. The truth is, I'm involved with someone else. And it's serious."

For a long moment, there was only silence on the other end of the phone. Finally, in a voice almost as icy as his mother's could be, she said, "I see. Well, it's your loss."

Then she hung up.

Matt looked at the phone, then returned it to its holder. Had he actually managed to get rid of her? He knew there would probably be repercussions as a result of their conversation, but he no longer cared.

He managed to put Charlotte and her phone call out of his mind and was deep into an analysis of a lengthy crime report when there was a knock at his office door, followed by the entrance of his sister.

He smiled in greeting. Of all his family, Madeleine was his favorite, the only one he felt completely comfortable with, the only one he felt loved him unconditionally. She looked wonderful, as always. Tall, slender, glowing with good health, she was the picture of the all-American girl with her long golden-brown hair, her large green eyes—a throwback to their great-grandmother Britton—and her bright smile. At twenty-seven, she was an accomplished and talented artist who worked for the largest advertising agency in Austin.

"What're you doing here?" he said, getting up to hug her.

"I have to give a presentation to a potential client at one o'clock and hoped I could persuade you to have an early lunch."

Matt thought about all the work he had to do and the fact he'd taken off early yesterday. "Nothing I'd like better," he said. "What did you have in mind?"

"You know me. I could eat Tex-Mex five times a week."

Ten minutes later, after a short walk, they were

seated at a window booth in a locally owned restaurant that happened to be one of Matt's favorites. After their waitress had given them their iced tea and set a basket of warm chips and a bowl of salsa on the table, Madeleine said, "What I really wanted to talk to you about is Mom."

"Not my favorite subject."

"I just can't believe what she's doing to Olivia."

"I know."

"It's just wrong, Matt. Olivia is a wonderful mother."

"I agree."

"She called me this morning and said her attorney filed an official petition with family court Friday afternoon."

Damn. Matt had figured this was coming, but it was still a blow. He wondered if Olivia knew yet. They had only talked on the phone over the weekend because she and Thea spent the weekend in Dallas with friends where Thea enjoyed Halloween festivities and Olivia had been able to forget, at least for a little while, what was happening at home.

"Can't you talk to Mom?" Madeleine said.

"I've tried. It doesn't do any good. Reason doesn't work with our mother. Not where Liv is concerned."

Madeleine shook her head. "This whole thing is just crazy."

"It is, but now that she's set this in motion, our mother will see it through to the bitter end, no matter who she hurts or how much harm she does."

"And there's nothing you can do? I mean, couldn't you talk to the people at family court? Pull some strings?"

"I wish I could, Maddie, but Mom and Dad have a hotshot attorney and now that they've made their charge official, everything is set in motion. At this point, the only way it would stop is if they changed their minds and withdrew their petition. And trust me, there's not a snowball's chance in hell of that happening."

Madeleine's eyes clouded. "I feel so bad for Olivia."

"Yeah. Me, too."

"I want to testify on her behalf."

"I figured you would." He reached across the table and took her hand, giving it a squeeze. "You sure you can handle the fallout? It won't be pretty."

"I can handle it."

"Good. I intend to testify on Olivia's behalf, too."

"Oh, I never doubted *that*."

Something about his sister's tone told him she suspected how he felt about Olivia. He gave her a quizzical look.

"C'mon, Matt. It's obvious how you feel about her. At least, to me it is."

He started to answer, but just then their waitress brought their food: fish tacos for Madeleine, the house enchiladas for Matt. With unspoken agreement, they waited till the waitress was out of earshot before resuming their conversation.

"Does Olivia know how you feel?" Madeleine asked as she picked up one of her tacos.

So even though he'd never intended to say anything to anyone about what had happened between him and Olivia, especially last Wednesday night, he found himself telling Madeleine everything.

Her eyes were filled with sympathy when he finished. "You can't blame her for wanting calm instead of constant storms, Matt," she said softly. "If Mom wasn't my mother, I wouldn't want any part of her, either."

He sighed. "I don't blame Olivia. I understand. Hell,

don't you think *I'd* like some peace and quiet for a change? Dealing with our mother is like picking your way through a minefield every day. You never know when something is going to explode under your feet."

Because the subject of Vivienne had depressed them both, Matt asked his sister what was new in her life, and she gave him an update while they ate. Afterward, they walked back to his building and hugged goodbye.

"Call me if you need me," Madeleine said.

"I will."

"I love you, big brother."

"Ditto, kid."

Madeleine waved and headed to the parking lot and her car, and Matt went inside. Once he was settled at his desk, he called Olivia.

She answered the phone almost immediately. He could hear squeals and giggling in the background.

"You're at home," he said. "I thought you'd be at work."

"I'm on the four-to-midnight shift this week. I have to drop Thea at day care soon."

"She sounds happy. What's she doing?" He knew he was stalling, but he hated to give her the news about the petition if she didn't already know it.

"Playing with the kitten we picked out this morning."

"I thought maybe you'd changed your mind."

"No, I couldn't do that. She's so excited, Matt. Listen to her. And the kitten is so cute. Oh, and guess what she's named her?" Olivia was laughing.

"I have no idea."

"Kitty Kat!"

He made himself laugh, too, even though he felt murderous. Damn his mother. Olivia should always be laughing. "Well, it makes sense."

"It does, doesn't it? I'm spelling *cat* with a *K*, though."

"Send me a picture."

"Okay. I will."

He couldn't put off telling her any longer. "I hate to bring up bad news, but has Austin called?"

"About your parents filing their petition Friday?"

"So he did call."

"Yes. Last night."

"Did he explain the next step will be for a caseworker to come and interview you? Inspect your home?"

"Yes."

When she didn't say anything more, he realized she didn't want to talk about this while Thea was in hearing distance. "You okay?" he asked softly.

"I'm fine. Resigned. Besides, I've got a more immediate problem."

"Oh?"

"Yeah, my mom always picks Thea up at day care when I fill in for the afternoon shift, and today she can't. Eve was always my backup, so now I guess I need to call Stella and see if she can do it."

Matt made a quick decision. "Don't call Stella. I'll pick Thea up. What time do I need to be there?"

"No, Matt, I don't want you to have to do that. I can—"

"I don't *have* to do it. I want to do it. I'm her godfather, remember? What time?"

She started to protest again, and he interrupted her a second time. "C'mon, Olivia. This is not a big deal. In fact, it'll be fun for me. What time should I be there?"

"Um, around five thirty? Is that too early?"

"Five thirty is fine," Matt said, already mentally juggling his schedule. He could bring work home with him, do some reading after Thea was asleep. "Will you let the day care center know I'm coming?"

"If you're sure…" She still sounded doubtful.

"I'm sure."

"Okay, I'll call the director and tell her you'll be there."

"Good."

"But, Matt, I won't be home until after midnight."

"No problem. I'll enjoy having Thea to myself. We'll have fun. She likes pizza, doesn't she?"

"She *loves* pizza. No meat, but lots of cheese."

"A girl after my own heart."

"Don't forget, you'll have the kitten, too. And the litter box."

"Not a big deal. Remember, you're talking to a criminal prosecutor."

"Thea will want the kitten to sleep with her."

"Is that all right with you?"

He could hear her resigned sigh. "I guess."

"So we're good?"

She finally agreed, saying, "I'll write some instructions and put them on the counter in the kitchen. And I'll leave a key for you out back. I'll put that in Thea's little red bucket. In her sandbox."

Matt smiled. He'd like to see the burglar who could figure *that* one out. "Good. We're all set."

Her voice softened. "I'll owe you one, Matt."

He waited a heartbeat, then answered just as softly, "I've told you before that I'd do anything for you, Liv. You *and* Thea. Don't you believe me?"

For a moment, he didn't think she was going to answer. Then, in a whisper so soft, he nearly missed it, she said, "Yes, I believe you."

And then she disconnected the call.

* * *

She shouldn't have agreed to let Matt pick up Thea. What was wrong with her that she couldn't stick to her decisions? She knew there was no future for her and Matt. She knew it was best she distance herself from him. Yet at the first small problem, what did she do? Like a drowning woman, she latched on to Matt as if he were the only life preserver around. She was hopeless.

What she should do, like it or not, was quit her job and stay home and be Vivienne's version of a proper mother to Thea. If she'd done that in the beginning, and not gone back to work until Thea started school, she wouldn't have to worry about Vivienne and her accusations. In fact, Vivienne wouldn't have a leg to stand on.

Even if Olivia didn't quit entirely, she could stop filling in for the afternoon shift when they were short-handed. So what if she got paid extra when she did so? It wasn't as if she was financially destitute. She had Mark's insurance money, after all. Yes, she wanted to keep it intact for Thea's education and more, but if she had to use some of it to ensure Thea had a stable, happy childhood, it wouldn't be the end of the world, would it?

Around and around Olivia's thoughts went after her conversation with Matt. Several times, she almost called him back to say she'd changed her mind and wouldn't need his help, after all.

But then Eve called, and after they talked, she felt better. She always felt better when she talked to Eve, who seemed able to put things into perspective when Olivia was looking at them too emotionally. By the time they ended their conversation, Olivia had settled down and decided to let things stand the way they were.

But tonight, when she saw Matt again, she needed to make sure he understood their relationship couldn't be a romantic one. She had to be strong, no matter how much she wished circumstances were different.

Because if she *wasn't* strong, if she yielded to her loneliness and the growing desire between them, she was just asking for more heartache.

The first thing Olivia saw when she walked into the kitchen after work that night was the gorgeous vase of flowers sitting in the center of the kitchen table. For a moment, she thought they were from Matt, but then he entered the kitchen and said, "I brought them in from your front stoop. I guess the florist thought it was okay to leave them there."

"Oh. Thank you." Olivia frowned. Who on earth had sent them? And why? It wasn't her birthday…or any other kind of holiday. She eyed the card.

"Go ahead," Matt said, giving her a crooked smile. "Read the card."

Olivia hesitated the briefest of seconds. She wished Matt wasn't standing there. His presence made her feel self-conscious. She wished she could casually say, *Oh, the flowers can wait, how'd things go with Thea?* Yet she couldn't. So with an inward, resigned sigh, she reached for the envelope containing the card.

It wasn't sealed. Had Matt already read it? Her heart picked up speed. No, he wouldn't do that. He was too much of a straight arrow. He would never violate her privacy.

She opened the card.

Don't let Friday's events upset you. We will prevail.
Austin

Looking up from the card, her eyes met Matt's. She swallowed, putting the card back in its envelope. Now her heart was beating hard.

"The flowers are from Austin Crenshaw, aren't they?" he said.

She nodded.

"See? I knew he viewed you as more than a client."

"He...he's just trying to make me feel better. Not worry." Why was she sounding so apologetic? She hadn't done anything wrong.

"I'm sure he is."

"It... The flowers don't mean anything." Oh, why had she said *that*? She was an idiot. She never knew when to be quiet. Her heart sped up as their gazes locked. Why did Matt have to look so sexy standing there? He still wore his work clothes, but he was barefoot and he'd taken off his tie and rolled up his shirtsleeves.

"We both know that's not true, Olivia."

Because she was so flustered, but mainly because her wildly conflicting emotions and lack of willpower where Matt was concerned frightened her, she went on the defensive. "Why are we even discussing this, Matt? It's not important. They're just flowers. Here. You can read the card. It's perfectly professional." She thrust the card into Matt's hand.

He didn't even look at it. Just placed it on the table behind her. Then, looking deep into her eyes, he pulled her into his arms.

She couldn't look away. She could barely breathe.

"Why are you so mad?" he said.

She swallowed. What could she say? The truth? *I don't know what to do or say because I want you so badly. I want what isn't possible.*

For a long moment the only sounds in the room were the ticking of the clock on the wall and their own breathing.

Still holding her gaze, he said, "I want to kiss you, Olivia. If you don't want me to, say so now."

"I—" She stopped, unable to continue. To say no would be lying. Of course, she wanted him to kiss her. She'd been wanting that ever since she'd admitted to herself how she felt about him. The one kiss he *had* given her hadn't been nearly enough. It had only whet her appetite for more. Much more. *Don't do this. It's foolhardy.*

"So it's okay?" he said.

Dear Heaven. Knowing she was lost, her eyes answered for her. And when his lips met hers, she sighed deeply, opening her mouth and her heart to him. Every sensible and rational objection she might have made was buried under an avalanche of feeling, a torrent of emotion and desire and need and loneliness. The kiss went on and on, overpowering everything except how much she loved and wanted this man.

When his hands dropped down to cup her bottom and pull her closer, she felt his heat, and her body responded with a fire of its own.

"I want you so much," he muttered, burying his face in her neck. "I wish—"

"Don't talk," she whispered. "Just make love to me."

"But I don't have a condom with me. I didn't expect—"

"It doesn't matter," she said, yielding to the moment, rationalizing it through her emotions, feeling rather than reasoning that if this was the only chance she'd ever have to be with Matt, she was going to take it. Besides, she knew she wasn't ovulating. Her period was due to start in two days.

Grabbing his hand, she pulled him toward the hall and her little study, where there was a daybed. She wouldn't take him upstairs, not with Thea asleep in the bedroom next to hers.

"Are you sure?" he said, giving her one more chance to back out.

"I said, don't talk."

Later, she wouldn't remember getting undressed. Somehow, in the middle of all the kissing, they managed to shed their clothing, which ended up in puddles on the floor. And then they became a tangle of arms and legs on the daybed, with only the light from the hallway spilling into the room.

He was a wonderful lover—thoughtful and generous. He gave her body his full attention, kissing her everywhere, touching her and stroking her and exploring her. When she would have responded in kind, he whispered, "Not yet. Let me love you first."

So she closed her eyes and gave herself up to the sensations. She didn't allow herself to think, only feel. It felt so right to be there, to allow him to care for her the way he wanted to. When he finally turned his attention to that most intimate part of her, she gasped, and her body responded immediately. Her back arched, and it was all she could do not to cry out, especially as his fingers delved. She tried to push him away, not wanting to reach that peak without him, but he wouldn't allow her to. Instead, his mouth covered hers, shutting off her protest, and his fingers moved more urgently.

Her body, denied release for so long, built to a crescendo, then exploded. Waves and waves of intense pleasure pummeled her, leaving her breathless and so weak, she could barely move. And it was then, and only then, that he slowly entered her.

The feel of him, his strength and heat, caused her to gasp. And as he began to move, she felt her own strength returning, and she moved with him. Soon they found their rhythm and within moments, she could feel herself climbing once more, desire building to another peak, and when she felt him stiffen, then shudder as he reached his own release, she allowed herself to let go once again, and she held tightly to him and gave herself up to the painful pleasure of loving him.

Chapter Nine

Later, the two of them covered by the quilt she kept on the daybed, nestled spoon fashion in Matt's arms, Olivia knew this was where she belonged, the place where she felt safe and loved and protected, the place she always wanted to be. Yet nothing had changed, even though everything had changed.

"You're not sorry, are you?" Matt murmured, tightening his arms around her, kissing her shoulder.

"Never," she said. She sighed deeply, contentment in every pore. She could lie there, in his arms, forever. She didn't even care that his car was parked in her driveway. That her neighbors, if they happened to be awake, would know that at one o'clock in the morning, he was still at her house. And she knew she *should* care. Because if Vivienne should somehow find out… Well, that possibility didn't bear thinking about.

"What's wrong?" Matt asked.

"Nothing."

"Don't lie to me, Olivia. I felt you tense up. Something is bothering you. What?"

Sighing, she said, "Just your mother. What she'd do if she knew about us. About this."

"Maybe we should just tell her."

That statement made Olivia turn in his arms so she could look at him. "No, Matt. We can't do that."

"Why not? We haven't done anything wrong. And I certainly don't intend to pretend things are still the same between us. Not after tonight. I love you, Olivia. I want everyone to know that. I want to declare that love openly. I want to marry you."

His words thrilled her even as they terrified her. "But Matt, we can't do any of that. I—I'm not convinced there will ever be any kind of future for us, and telling the world right now, while this custody suit is going on, would be crazy. It's just asking for more trouble."

"What if we informed the judge who will handle the case that we intend to get married? It would be very hard for anyone, my mother included, to say Thea would be better off with her and Dad than with you and me."

Oh, it was tempting. But what if he was wrong? What if Vivienne already had the judge in her pocket? That wouldn't surprise Olivia, because Vivienne had boasted in the past about her powerful friends, and how she could get anything she wanted, whenever she wanted. And Olivia had seen her do just that. So had Matt.

"But Matt, you know how dangerous your mother is. Why give her more ammunition? We would be taking a terrible chance. I'm not willing to gamble with Thea in the crosshairs. We at least need to wait and see what happens with the custody case. If things go my way, then we can talk again. But in the meantime—"

His arms tightened around her. "Don't say we can't see each other again. I won't agree to that."

"Matt..."

"No, Olivia. There's not a thing wrong with us spending time together. Even my mother can't make that seem wrong, because it isn't. After all, we've always spent time together. We're family."

Because she hadn't the strength to keep arguing with him, Olivia let his reasoning go unchallenged, because essentially, he was right, yet inwardly, she couldn't rid herself of her foreboding. She knew some people might think she was paranoid where Vivienne was concerned, but that didn't make her fears any less real. But instead of saying anything more, she simply threw off the quilt and attempted to get up.

"Where are you going?" He tried to hold her back.

"I'm sorry, Matt, but it's late. It's time for you to leave and for me to go up to my bedroom. Thea sometimes wakes up in the night, and I don't want her to think I'm not here."

But instead of letting her go, he pulled her back. "I don't want to leave," he said softly.

"I know. I don't want you to, either. But you have to."

He sighed and finally released her.

Ten minutes later, both dressed again—and now he had his shoes and jacket on—she said goodbye to him at the front door. He kissed her lingeringly and held her close for a long moment. "I love you," he said again, resting his head against hers.

She understood he wanted to hear her say she loved him, too, and part of her wanted to say it, but something stopped her.

"I'll call you tomorrow."

"Okay."

After one last kiss, he said good-night, and walked out the door.

"I'm thinking of quitting my job." It was Wednesday morning and five days since the Brittons' petition had been filed in family court.

"But why?" Olivia's mother said.

"Because if I'm a stay-at-home mom, Vivienne's case against me will be a lot weaker."

"But, honey, you really like your job. And there's not a thing wrong with you working. After all, you're a single mother."

"I know that and you know that, but what's going on right now with Vivienne's case is more important. And once Thea starts kindergarten, maybe I can go back to school myself." This idea had come to her after Matt had gone home early Tuesday morning, and Olivia hadn't been able to fall asleep because she couldn't shut off her brain.

"You'd go into nursing?"

"Yes, I think so." When she'd become pregnant with Thea, Olivia had put her dream of becoming a nurse on hold. But now maybe becoming a registered nurse would be a possibility for her.

Her mother smiled. "That would actually be wonderful, I think. I mean, you talked about being a nurse from the time you were about five years old."

"I know." Olivia smiled, too. "And once Thea's in school, I'd have the freedom to do that." She wondered what Matt would think of her idea, and had a feeling he would like it. In fact, she couldn't imagine Matt preventing her from doing anything she wanted to do. He simply wasn't like that.

"Have you talked to Eve about this?"

"Not yet. Why?"

"Well, I know from what Anna has said, that Eve hopes you'll move out to LA and work for Adam."

"She told her mother that?"

"Yes."

"And you like the idea?" She wished she could see her mother's expression, but the two women were talking by phone while Norma was on her lunch break.

"Not really," her mother said, "but I wouldn't have made a fuss if that's what you truly wanted to do. I mean, the idea does have merit. A change might be really good for you, and removing Thea from Vivienne's constant interference would certainly make your life easier. And, as Anna pointed out, I could come out and visit you as often as I wanted."

Olivia couldn't believe her mother was actually advocating for such a radical change.

"I'm not saying I think you should move, honey. I'm just saying if you wanted to, I wouldn't make it difficult for you. I want what's best for both you and Thea, you know that."

"I do know it, and I love you for it." Olivia thought, not for the first time, how lucky she was to have a mother like Norma. To have a family who loved her and only wanted the best for her.

And now you have Matt, too.

If only Matt wasn't a Britton. If only he, too, had a family like hers.

She wondered if she should tell her mother what had happened between them. Not about the sex, of course. That was private. But about the fact that Matt had proposed to her. That she loved him, too, even though she hadn't told him.

Yet something stopped her. And it wasn't just that they were talking on the telephone and this seemed news that should be discussed in person. Mostly, she said nothing because maybe it was too soon. Maybe, as she'd advised Matt, she should wait till this whole custody thing was over. Once that was behind her, once she no longer had that to fear from Vivienne, then she'd confide in her mother.

"So you're okay with picking Thea up tonight?" she said instead.

"I'll be there."

"I love you, Mom."

"I love you more."

Olivia was smiling as she disconnected the call.

Olivia had only been on her shift for a little more than an hour when her cell rang. She didn't recognize the number, so she let the call go to voice mail. She could deal with it on her break.

The call turned out to be from the caseworker assigned to do a home evaluation and interview with her prior to the hearing at family court. The woman, whose name was Joan Barwood, left a number for Olivia to call. Taking a deep breath, telling herself there was nothing to fear, Olivia placed the call.

"Joan Barwood."

"Hello, Ms. Barwood. This is Olivia Britton returning your call."

"Yes, hello, Mrs. Britton. I was calling to see if we could set up a convenient time for me to come and visit your home and talk with you and Thea."

"I'm free every morning for the next three days."

"How about Friday at ten, then?"

"That's perfect. You have my address?"

"I do."

"And you want Thea to be there?"

"Yes, I do."

"All right. I'll see you then."

Olivia's hands were shaking when she disconnected the call. She had promised to call Austin and let him know when she'd been contacted. He answered almost immediately.

"I'm glad you've heard from the caseworker," he said. "I was hoping they'd visit quickly, not make you wait."

"Yes, I'm glad to get it over with quickly, too," she agreed.

"I'll check on Ms. Barwood tomorrow. See what I can find out about her. I'll call you after I do."

"That would be great, Austin." She would also ask Matt what he might know about the woman. "Oh, and I meant to tell you, thank you so much for the beautiful flowers. That was very thoughtful of you."

"I'm glad you like them. And listen, don't worry too much, okay? You'll do fine with the Barwood woman. Just be yourself. She won't be able to help liking you."

"I'll try. It's just that the whole idea is nerve-racking. That some stranger is coming into your home to evaluate it…and you."

"I know. But try to relax. She's a professional. Trained to be objective. It's not like she's your mother-in-law's paid assassin or anything."

"I know." But Olivia couldn't help feeling that the unknown Ms. Barwood might actually be just that. Perhaps she was someone Vivienne already knew and had already influenced.

"You don't sound very convinced."

Olivia sighed. "I'm sorry. I'm trying. It's just that all of this is so scary. This woman could hold my fate, Thea's fate, in her hands."

"She's not going to give you a bad report. How could she? You don't do drugs. You don't leave Thea alone. You don't run around or hang out in bars. You've never been arrested. You work in an honest profession. You have a close family. And Thea is obviously a healthy, well-adjusted, happy child."

"Yet her grandmother says I'm an unfit mother. And supposedly has proof." She still had no idea what this so-called proof was.

"Vivienne Britton is just used to getting her own way. And threatening people has always worked for her."

Olivia nodded, then felt silly because of course, he couldn't see her. "I know."

"But it's not going to work now," he said firmly.

"No." But even though she said it, she couldn't help feeling scared.

"Look, I've dealt with people like her…and worse than her…since Adam's career took off the way it has. She's a bully. I know how to handle bullies."

They talked awhile longer, then just as she was about to say goodbye, he said, "Let me take you to dinner Friday night. We can go over everything."

"Oh, Austin, I'm sorry. I can't. Friday is my last day on the afternoon shift."

"Saturday, then."

"Um, I just—"

"Don't say no, Olivia. It'll be the perfect way for us to catch up on everything. You can tell me how the home inspection went and we can go over our strategy for court."

She really didn't want to go, not after what had happened with Matt, but she didn't know how to get out of it gracefully, either, because she certainly couldn't tell Austin the truth. So she finally agreed, and he said he'd pick her up at seven.

She sighed after they hung up. She hoped her mother would be able to babysit again. It seemed as if Olivia was always asking her, and that didn't seem very fair. If Vivienne wasn't doing what she was doing, Olivia would have called *her*, but of course, now that option was out of the question. Maybe she should call Austin back and tell him to just plan on having dinner there at the house, with her and Thea. No, not a good idea. Thing was, if they were out to dinner, she could more easily control the length of time they spent together. If he was there, in her home, it would be hard for her to end the evening if he seemed the least bit reluctant to leave. Maybe she should just ask Stella.

Stella was always her last choice because, after all, Stella was young and had a life of her own. She loved Thea wholeheartedly and she never acted reluctant to help out, but Olivia knew she could easily take advantage of Stella's good nature and generosity, and she never wanted to do that. Especially since there was little she could ever do for Stella in return. However, "needs must" as Olivia's grandmother Dubrovnik always used to say.

Before she changed her mind, she placed the call to her sister.

"Hey," Stella said. "What's up?"

"Sorry to bother you at work, but I need a sitter for Saturday night. You available?"

"You're in luck. I am. Why don't you let Thea come to my place and spend the night?"

Olivia smiled. "She'd love that, but, um, I have a bit of a problem, and it would be better if you were here."

"Why's that?"

"Austin Crenshaw is taking me to dinner, and I don't want to come back here to an empty house. If you're here, he won't suggest coming in."

"Olivia…"

"What?"

"Austin Crenshaw is *hot*. Most women would give their right arm to go out with him. And invite him in afterward."

"I'm not most women. And Austin is my attorney."

"So?"

"Mixing business with pleasure is not smart."

"Oh, c'mon. It's not like the two of you work together, or anything. He's just handling your case, which will soon be over."

"I'm just… I'm not interested in him that way. And I'd like to avoid potential awkwardness on Saturday."

"Why aren't you interested in him? Are you blind?"

"No. I realize he's attractive and sexy and all that, but you know, I'm just not…interested," she finished lamely.

"All right, if that's your final word. But I think you're nuts."

"That's my final word. Besides, don't you need to get back to work?" Stella was a sales rep for a software-related company.

Stella laughed. "Nice way to change the subject. Okay, fine. What time do you need me on Saturday?"

"Can you come by at six?"

"Sure."

"Thanks, Stella. I'll owe you one."

"Yes, you will."

After exchanging "I love you," the sisters hung up.

Olivia sat there for a long moment, then, with a sigh, placed her final call.

"Good morning," Matt said when he answered.

She couldn't help smiling. "Yes, it is."

"If you're calling to thank me, it's not necessary."

"Thank you? For what?"

He chuckled softly. "For great sex?"

"Matt!" She could actually feel herself blushing.

"What? My door's closed. No one can hear me. And it *was* great, wasn't it?"

"Yes, it was." Her stupid heart was beating too fast.

"Maybe we could have a repeat performance."

Now she laughed. "I told you. We have to be cool. We can't do anything to jeopardize the custody suit. Which brings me to the real reason I called. The caseworker phoned me. She's going to come and do her interview and home inspection Friday morning."

"Good. Glad it'll soon be over."

"I thought maybe you could check her out for me. See what kind of reputation she has."

"What's her name?"

"Joan Barwood."

"I've heard of her. I'll do some checking today and call you later."

"Okay. Thanks."

"So when is the afternoon shift over?"

"Friday's my last day. I have the weekend off, then go back on days Monday."

"How about letting me take you and Thea somewhere fun on Saturday?"

"Matt, I don't think that's a good idea. Besides, I have a prior commitment on Saturday." She hoped he wouldn't ask what the commitment was because she didn't want to lie to him, but she also wasn't in the mood for any kind of argument.

"How about Sunday, then?"

"What did you have in mind?"

"Maybe a picnic at the park. Or we could drive to San Antonio, take a boat ride on the river, have some good Mexican food. Maybe look around at El Mercado."

Because Vivienne wasn't likely to hear about a visit to San Antonio, and Olivia loved going there, she agreed to this plan, and Matt said he'd come by and pick them up around ten.

By the time their phone conversation was over, it was time for her to get ready for work. Hopefully, when she got there, it would be so busy she wouldn't have time to worry about anything.

Chapter Ten

For at least the tenth time, Olivia checked the house to make sure she'd left nothing undone. The furniture shone with polish, the floors were immaculate, the air smelled fragrant with the scent of freshly brewed coffee mixed with the tempting richness of the pumpkin muffins she'd taken from the oven only minutes earlier, and Thea was happily playing with her dollhouse—a birthday gift from Eve and the twins.

Everything was ready for the caseworker's visit.

The thought had no sooner formed than the doorbell rang. Olivia's heart knocked painfully. She took a deep breath before going forward to answer the door. *There's nothing to be nervous about. Just be honest and straightforward with the woman. You have nothing to fear.*

So why then did she feel as if she were headed to the guillotine? Actually, she knew why. It was because so much was at stake. If this interview went well, the Barwood woman would recommend the court let Thea remain with her mother. If it didn't go well, who knew what could happen?

Forcing herself to smile normally, Olivia opened the door. Standing on the stoop was a tall, thin woman with a narrow face, wispy brownish-blond hair pulled back into a tiny bun and a too-long nose. She was dressed in a drab brown skirt, white blouse and olive green jacket. Olivia's heart sank. The woman didn't inspire confidence.

"Hi," Olivia said. "I'm Olivia Britton. And you're…"

"Joan Barwood," the caseworker said. She smiled.

The smile changed her face, made her seem much warmer and friendlier. Olivia's spirits lifted a fraction. "Come in," she invited.

The Barwood woman stepped inside and looked around. "Lovely," she said. "I liked the look of the house from the outside, too. Small but inviting."

"Yes, that's what Mark and I thought when we bought the house. It looked like a happy family would live in it." The memory caused Olivia a twinge of sadness, but she shook it off. "May I take your jacket?"

"Thank you." Joan Barwood removed the jacket and handed it to Olivia, who hung it in the tiny coat closet in the foyer.

"I thought we could sit in the living room," Olivia said, gesturing toward the open doorway to Ms. Barwood's left.

"It would be easier if we sat at the kitchen table. I have forms that need to be filled out as we talk." Ms. Barwood looked into the living room as she spoke. "Oh, I see your daughter is playing in there."

Olivia smiled. "Yes. Thea, honey? Come out and

meet Mommy's friend." She breathed a sigh of relief when Thea immediately obeyed. Lately, it wasn't a certainty that she would. She'd begun showing quite a streak of independence.

"Hi," Thea said, grinning up at Ms. Barwood. "I'm Thea. I'm four years old."

"I can see that. Quite a big girl, aren't you?"

Thea nodded proudly. "I look like my daddy."

"Do you? Well, you seem to have your mommy's eyes."

"But I have his hair and his nose and his ears."

Joan Barwood smiled. "He must have been a very nice-looking man, your father, because you're a very pretty little girl."

"I know," Thea said.

Both Olivia and Joan Barwood chuckled at the remark.

"She's not shy, I see," Joan Barwood said. Her pale blue eyes met Olivia's.

"No. Not in the least. In fact, sometimes she's too friendly. I've been warning her about that tendency."

"Mommy says I shouldn't talk to strangers," Thea said. "But I like talking to people. They're inner-esting."

"Interesting," Olivia said.

Thea gave her a long-suffering look and sighed dramatically. "That's what I *said*, Mommy."

"A mind of her own, too, I see," Joan Barwood said.

"Yes," Olivia said. "Thea, why don't you go back to playing with your dollhouse while Ms. Barwood and I go into the kitchen to talk."

"Okay." But Thea seemed reluctant, because she frowned a little. But she turned and went back to her toys.

"This way," Olivia said.

A few minutes later, with Joan Barwood settled at the kitchen table, her paperwork on the table in front of her, Olivia poured two cups of coffee and brought them, plus a small pitcher of half-and-half and a bowl of sugar to the table. "I have fresh muffins," she offered. "They're still warm."

"No, thank you," Joan Barwood said. Then, softening a bit, she added, "Maybe later."

Olivia sat across from her. Their eyes met again.

"I like your home," the caseworker said. "Is it paid for? Or do you have a mortgage?"

"It's paid for. Mark bought a separate insurance policy to cover it, just in case." Olivia thought about how she'd argued against doing that because the premiums were so high. But when Mark had been killed, she'd been very grateful to him for his thoughtfulness.

"That was smart."

"Yes, he was pretty sensible when it came to me."

"And you have a full-time job?"

"I do. At the Crandall Lake Hospital. I'm in Admitting."

"On the day shift, right?"

"Yes, but I do fill in for the afternoon shift when they're shorthanded."

"Is that a requirement of the job?"

"No, but it pays time and a half, so that really helps financially. My mother watches Thea when I take those shifts."

Barwood nodded thoughtfully. "But I would have thought your husband left you quite well off. I mean, the Britton family is very wealthy."

"Yes, but that's his parents. Mark had other insurance—aside from the policy that paid off the house—and it was substantial, and Thea gets social security until she's eighteen, but my working is really helpful. I really hope to keep his insurance intact for Thea. To finance her education, and to help her get a good start in life when she's older."

"That's commendable, but surely the complainant, her Britton grandparents, would provide for her, if necessary? She's their only grandchild, isn't that correct?"

"Yes, that's true. But—" Olivia hesitated, then plunged ahead. She had to be honest. She didn't know any other way *to* be. "But if they were paying, they would want to control everything. As Thea's mother, I'd have no say. And frankly, Ms. Barwood, I'm not sure Thea would, either. I don't want that for my daughter. I want her to continue to grow up strong and independent, and to form her own ideas and opinions, not be told how to live and what to think."

Now that Olivia had begun to explain, she couldn't seem to stop. "Anyway, Thea loves going to day care. And I don't think it's harmful. She's learned to share and get along with other children. She's very social, and she's made so many friends."

Joan Barwood nodded, then made some notes on her forms. When finished, she looked up again. "The complainant, your in-laws, have stated that you aren't as careful about Thea's welfare as you should be. That she fell and split her lip last year and had to have stitches because you had left her alone in your backyard."

"I didn't leave her alone. I simply walked into the kitchen to get the sandwiches I'd made for our lunch. I wasn't inside for more than two minutes."

Glancing again at her notes, Barwood said, "Yet in that two minutes, she fell and cut her lip and knocked out a tooth."

Olivia sighed. She still remembered how frightened

she'd been when she'd seen the blood gushing from Thea's mouth. "Yes, but accidents happen. I wasn't neglecting her. Why, her father told me that he once fell off the sliding board in his backyard. Actually, he said he jumped. He thought he was Superman because he was wearing a Superman cape. Was that his mother's fault? I mean, she was sitting right there and she couldn't stop him falling and hurting himself. He broke his arm! Had to wear a cast for weeks."

"I don't know the circumstances of Thea's father's accident. But we're not discussing that. We're discussing what happened to Thea."

Olivia should have known that episode would be on Vivienne's list of grievances against her. "What else do my in-laws say about me?" she said, trying not to sound bitter.

Barwood consulted her notes again. "They mention an incident last year where Thea darted into the street where she could have been struck by a car."

Olivia wanted to scream. Vivienne had been out of sorts that entire day because it was Thea's birthday and she'd wanted to have an elaborate party for her at the Britton home. But for once, Olivia had stood up to her mother-in-law and held the celebration at her mother's house. "Did they also mention that they were both with us at the time? And that Thea had spied a baby rabbit? And that none of us were able to grab her in time to prevent her running after it?"

Barwood's eyes again met Olivia's. "No. That detail isn't here."

"Well, they were. And I immediately went after Thea and caught her before any harm came to her." She'd brought her back to their group kicking and screaming, but Olivia decided not to say so. Thea's stubbornness was an ongoing problem, and would probably only get worse as she got older. She was a strong-willed child; she would cause Olivia to become prematurely gray, Olivia was sure of it. Yet Olivia wouldn't have her any other way.

"Let's talk about Thea's eating habits," the Barwood woman said after making a few more notes.

"Oh, brother," Olivia said, rolling her eyes.

"Is there a problem?" Joan Barwood said.

Olivia just shook her head. "No. Not for me or for Thea. But I should have known Vivienne would bring up my daughter's food preferences."

"Such as?"

"Well, she doesn't like meat. She's pretty much a vegetarian."

"What about you?"

"I'm not. I like just about everything, and I've tried to get her to at least taste things, but she's got a mind of her own, that one." Actually, not for the first time, Olivia thought that Thea's strong opinions were directly related to the genes she'd received from her paternal grandmother.

"So she doesn't eat any meat at all?"

"No. She likes fish, though, and she gets plenty of protein in beans and nuts and dairy. She has a very healthy diet, despite what my mother-in-law thinks."

Joan Barwood nodded thoughtfully. After glancing at her notes again, she said, "The day care issue seems to be primary. That, and the odd hours you sometimes work. Your in-laws feel Thea would be much better off in their home, with a normal, structured schedule, under the proper guidance of a full-time nanny."

"They're entitled to their opinion, but I don't agree. Thea belongs here, with me, her mother. But if my working really is a major issue, and you agree with that, then I'll quit immediately. Nothing in the world is more important to me than my daughter. Nothing."

The caseworker's eyes met hers. "I worked when my children were small," she finally said.

Olivia breathed a mental sigh of relief. Surely the Barwood woman was telling her something without actually telling her. Wasn't she?

They talked awhile longer, and then Ms. Barwood asked to see the rest of the house, and Olivia showed her around. The woman spent the longest time in Thea's bedroom, looking around, opening the closet door, the drawers to Thea's chest and small dresser, and her toy box. "It's a lovely room," she finally said.

Just as they were ready to go back downstairs, Thea appeared in the doorway. "Why are you in my room?" she demanded.

"Miss Barwood just wanted to see it, honey," Olivia said. "Because I told her how pretty it was."

"It is pretty," Joan Barwood agreed.

"I like it a lot," Thea said, frowning.

"What's wrong?" Ms. Barwood asked.

"It's *my* room." Now Thea's frown grew darker.

Olivia almost smiled. Her daughter was showing her colors right now. And her possessiveness.

"This is where my mommy tells me the daddy story," Thea said. The statement was almost challenging.

"The daddy story?" Ms. Barwood said.

"At night. When I go to sleep," Thea said.

"I always tell her how her daddy is looking out for her, and how much he loves her," Olivia said. She kept her voice neutral, but inside she was angry. Angry that she had to share something so intimate. Something that was no one's business except hers and her daughter's.

Angry that Vivienne had brought this unjustified ugliness into their lives.

"He's my *garden angel*!" Thea said, glaring at Joan Barwood.

The caseworker nodded. Then she knelt down, and took Thea's hand. "I'm sorry if I upset you, Thea. I can see you love your daddy and mommy very much, and that the daddy story is very important to you. Thank you for telling me about it."

Thea's frown slowly disappeared. "You're welcome."

"Such a polite little girl, too," Ms. Barwood said. "Your mommy has done a good job, that's very clear."

Olivia wasn't sure what to say…or do. But Joan Barwood obviously realized this, for she rose, then turned to Olivia and said, "I've enjoyed visiting both you and Thea, Olivia. Thank you for having me. Now I think it's time to get going."

Five minutes later, she was gone. After shutting the door behind her, Olivia felt as if the weight of the world had been lifted from her shoulders. No matter what the Barwood woman recommended, and Olivia was pretty certain the interview had gone well, Olivia was just glad to have this part of the custody suit behind her.

Now all she could do was wait.

After Olivia told him about the interview with the caseworker from Children's Protective Services, Matt decided to do some digging of his own. Knowing Paul Temple, the lawyer he'd wanted Olivia to use instead of Austin, would have inside knowledge of the way CPS worked, he called him to see what he could find out.

"I know Joan Barwood," Temple said. "She's one of the old hands in the department, very thorough, very conscientious and fair."

"Do you know her well enough to ask her about Olivia's case?"

There was a pause on the other end of the line. "I wouldn't normally do that," Temple finally said.

"As a favor to me?"

Another pause. Then a sigh, clearly audible. "Okay, Matt. As a favor to you."

"I'll owe you, Paul," Matt said.

"Yes, you will."

Less than an hour later, Paul Temple called him back. "I just spoke to Joan Barwood. She was hesitant to say anything, but when I pressed her, she admitted that your sister-in-law made a good impression on her. She'll give her a positive recommendation, I'm sure of it."

Matt hadn't even realized he'd been holding his breath until he let it out. "Thanks, Paul. I really appreciate this."

"Don't ask again."

Matt grinned. "I won't."

"I think a couple of bottles of a good red would be a nice payback, don't you?"

Now Matt laughed. "You got it."

After hanging up, he decided while he was out this afternoon would be a good time to make a call on his mother. Maybe, if she knew CPS wasn't going to be on her side, she'd drop this ridiculous custody suit before it went any further. It was worth a try, anyway.

He wouldn't give her any warning. He would just drop by the house on his way back from court. It was nearly three thirty before he pulled into the driveway at his parents' home. Luckily, his mother was in.

"Hello, Matthew," she said coolly.

"Mom," he said, bending over and kissing her cheek.

As usual, he caught the subtle fragrance of Beautiful, her perfume of choice.

"What's on your mind today?" she asked. Still no smile.

"I received some information I thought you might like to know." He kept his voice as pleasant as he could manage.

She lifted her chin. "Oh?"

"CPS sent a caseworker to Olivia's home this morning, and knowing Olivia, I'm certain the woman will give her a favorable recommendation. Are you sure you want to risk that?"

His mother's eyes narrowed, her jaw hardened.

"I thought maybe, under the circumstances, you might be persuaded to drop the custody suit and spare all of us the embarrassment of a public display of dirty family laundry."

"I believe I'll wait and see for myself what CPS has to say. And if they are so misguided as to be taken in by *that woman*, I'm sure Jackson Moyer will have more than one way to counter."

Matt sighed. He wasn't really surprised. His mother rarely backed down from a fight, mainly because she was always so convinced she was right and everyone else was wrong, but he'd felt he owed it to Olivia to at least make one more attempt to end this debacle. "I'm sorry to hear that."

"And I'm sorry to hear that you're still defending Olivia. I don't know how someone as intelligent as you can be taken in by her, but obviously you don't have any more sense where she's concerned than your brother did. He, at least, was *young*, and the young can be forgiven for foolish choices. But *you*, Matthew, should know better."

By now Matt was sorry he'd ever stopped by. He should have known better. His mother wasn't going to back down. Deciding he wouldn't be drawn into a lengthy argument, he turned to go, but her next words stopped him.

"Perhaps you thought I wasn't serious when I said I would withdraw my support for your candidacy for the US Senate."

Looking back at her, he said, "Oh, no. I knew you were serious."

"Good."

"Doesn't matter. I no longer intend to run for that seat."

Her face darkened. "Excuse me?"

"You heard me."

"You would thwart me? Even in this?"

"Thwart *you*? I swear, you live in another world."

"You're doing this out of some kind of misplaced spite. You know how much I wanted this for you."

"For *me*? Come on. That's a joke. You wanted that for *Mark*. You wanted it for *you*. Nothing in this house has ever been about me. From the moment Mark was born, it was like I'd never existed." All the bitterness and loneliness and hurt stored up in Matt over the years brimmed over and the words poured out. "So don't pretend otherwise, because I don't believe you."

Her mouth actually dropped open.

He almost laughed. But it wasn't funny. Nothing in this house had ever been funny.

"You're a fool," she finally said.

He almost told her then about Carter's offer, but an innate sense of self-preservation stopped him. She was entirely capable of calling the governor, with whom she was on a first-name basis, and attempting to ruin that for him, too. "Maybe so," he said softly. "But at least I can look at myself in the mirror every morning and not be ashamed of what I see."

And with that, he walked out the door and didn't look back.

Chapter Eleven

Austin arrived promptly at seven on Saturday. When Olivia opened the door, her first thought was that he was the kind of date most women would be thrilled to have. Her second was that this wasn't *really* a date, but she still hoped Matt didn't find out about tonight's dinner. Then she was mad at herself. Why shouldn't Matt know? And why hadn't she told him? She wasn't doing anything wrong. Austin was her lawyer, and it was completely reasonable that they should have dinner together. By not telling Matt, she was tacitly admitting she felt weird about the evening.

"You look lovely," Austin said, eyeing her wool dress with approval. "I like that shade of red."

She smiled. "It's called cranberry, in honor of the coming holidays."

"It looks good on you."

"Thank you." She reached for her black shawl and

small clutch bag, which she'd placed on the little table in the entryway.

"Where's Thea?" Austin said, looking around.

"At my sister's. Stella will bring her back here at bedtime and stay here till we get home." This had been a last-minute adjustment to their plans because Stella had a pitch to give to a potential client on Monday and wanted to do some last-minute work on it this evening without having to lug her laptop and other materials with her when she came to Olivia's.

Austin stood aside so she could precede him out the door. Soon she was settled in his Lexus and they were off.

"I made a reservation at Hugo's," Austin said.

Olivia raised her eyebrows. "Really?" Hugo's was a relatively new and already top tier restaurant in the lake district. The chef, a James Beard award winner, specialized in French cuisine with a Creole flair. "Wow."

Austin smiled. "I was hoping you'd be impressed."

Olivia didn't know how to respond. She knew he was subtly flirting, and she should be flattered, but instead she just felt even more uncomfortable than she had earlier.

When she didn't answer, his tone became more serious. "I was also hoping you'd be pleased."

"I am pleased, but—"

"What?"

Best to be honest. Or at least as honest as possible, under the circumstances. "I wasn't thinking of tonight as a date. I was thinking of it as a meeting. And Hugo's isn't a meeting sort of place." She made an effort to keep her voice light.

"And I was hoping tonight could be both," he said softly.

Olivia hesitated only a moment. "Until the custody issue is settled, I don't think it's appropriate for me to date anyone. I think I have to keep my head and my life clear of anything that could be construed as an obstacle to my winning."

"I see your point, but seriously, Olivia, I take my clients to lunch and dinner all the time. It's a perfect way to relax and talk and strategize."

"That may be true, but still, Hugo's?"

"All right. Here's the deal. We'll agree that this evening isn't a date. We won't get personal at all. We'll just talk about the case and anything else that might impact it. Does that work?"

Olivia nodded. "Yes. That works." But would he keep his promise? At a restaurant like Hugo's, it would be hard *not* to get personal. From what she'd heard, its entire ambiance invited confidences...and romance.

"Good. But that doesn't mean we can't enjoy wonderful food and a friendly glass of wine, does it?"

"N-no."

"So stop worrying and relax. We're almost there."

Her first impression of the restaurant was exactly what she'd expected: warmth mixed with elegance. It immediately welcomed you and soothed you. She had to admit she loved the atmosphere and the sense that everyone there cared only for your comfort and enjoyment. She sighed with pleasure as she sank into her softly upholstered chair and looked around. She particularly loved the floor-to-ceiling windows that gave diners a view of inviting tree-filled, lighted grounds.

"It's lovely," she told Austin.

"I'm glad you like it," he said, smiling.

Later, after receiving their glasses of Cabernet Sauvignon and placing their orders—the jumbo sea scallops for him, the mushroom risotto with lobster for her—he leaned back in his chair and said, "Now tell me about the home visit."

So she did. She also told him what Matt had found out about the Barwood woman, although she didn't tell him *how* he'd gotten the information.

"I knew the caseworker would like you."

Olivia couldn't help smiling at him. He really *was* so nice. "I'm still scared, though," she admitted. "Vivienne wields a big stick."

"Yes, I know that. Everyone living in Crandall Lake knows that. But her case for custody of Thea isn't strong. Not from what you've told me."

They continued to discuss the home visit and the things the Barwood woman had disclosed to Olivia until their food came. Both dishes were beautifully presented and smelled wonderful. Suddenly Olivia felt hungry and she was glad they'd come.

She had just fully relaxed and taken her second bite of the truly amazing risotto when a flash of red on her right caught her eye. Her heart jumped when she realized the red dress on the woman being seated across from them was worn by Catherine Elliott, one of Vivienne's bosom buddies. Catherine hadn't seen Olivia yet, but her husband, Arthur, had. He smiled and gave Olivia a little salute, causing Catherine to turn around curiously. When her dark eyes met Olivia's, she inclined her head, smiled slightly, and pointedly turned her curious gaze to Austin. Her expression changed the moment she realized who Olivia's escort was.

No, Olivia thought, her heart now sinking. But she kept her expression even and nodded a silent greeting. Then she turned her attention back to her dinner and tried to ignore the fear the presence of the Elliotts had generated.

Austin frowned. "What's wrong?"

Olivia forced herself not to show how disturbed she felt. "Don't look, but the couple just seated across from us are very good friends of my in-laws."

"So?"

"So Vivienne will now get a play-by-play description of our evening."

Austin shrugged. "We're having dinner, Olivia. We're not doing anything wrong. And I *am* your lawyer."

Olivia couldn't help but think how Matt had said the very same thing the other day about them not doing anything wrong. And even though both men were right, somehow Olivia knew Vivienne wouldn't see either situation the same way. Because, with Vivienne, even Olivia's breathing was a punishable offense.

She continued to eat her meal, but the lovely dinner now tasted like sawdust. Why had she agreed to come out with Austin? She knew that now Catherine Elliott would give Vivienne more ammunition to use against her, for no matter how innocent this dinner with Austin was, the two women would somehow make it seem otherwise.

"Stop worrying," Austin said.

But Olivia couldn't. She did manage to get most of her food down, but she refused dessert, and silently implored Austin to get her out of there. He sighed, and had just asked for the bill when Olivia's cell vibrated.

"I have to take this," she said, glancing at the screen and seeing that it was Stella. Excusing herself, she hurried in the direction of the ladies' room.

"Stella?" she said when she was out of earshot of the diners.

"Oh, thank goodness," Stella said. "Liv, I'm so sorry, but I had to call you. Something's happened."

Olivia's mouth went dry. "Is Thea all right?"

"Thea's fine, but…oh, God. We…there was a fire."

"A fire! Where?"

"In my building. We were just getting ready to leave to go to your house. I'd shut down my laptop and was packing my tote with my things. Thea was in the living room, and when I walked in there I smelled smoke. I couldn't imagine where it was coming from." Stella's words were tumbling out, tripping over each other. "For a minute, I thought I'd left the stove on or something, 'cause earlier I'd made her some hot chocolate. Then, a second later, I heard sirens and when I looked outside, I saw a fire truck coming into the parking lot along with emergency vehicles. I grabbed Thea and my tote and opened the apartment door to run out, but the hallway was already filled with smoke, and I couldn't see, so I shut the door again and stuffed my afghan under the door to keep the smoke out. Oh, God, Liv, I was so scared! My heart was just pounding like crazy! But we went out on the balcony where the firefighters could see us and they ended up rescuing us that way."

"The balcony!" Stella's apartment was on the third floor of her building. "Is Thea okay?"

"Yes, she's fine. She thought it was an adventure, actually. She wasn't afraid at all when the fireman took her down the ladder." Stella was calmer now that she'd gotten the story out.

"Ohmigod." Olivia was shaking, just thinking about it.

"She's okay, Liv, I promise. Not a scratch on her. And I'm fine, too, but the apartment building is a mess. The fire started in an apartment on the second floor, almost right below me. There was a lot of damage, both from the fire and the smoke. I don't know about my apartment, but I have a feeling it's pretty much a loss."

"Oh, God, Stell. I'm so sorry. But I'm grateful you're both okay." Olivia was trembling at the thought of what *could* have happened.

"Me, too. Thing is, looks like you or Mom are gonna have company for a while. I'm just grateful the firemen allowed me to take my tote bag with me when it was my turn to go down the ladder. And thank goodness my laptop was in it. If I'd lost that, I'd be in deep doo-doo."

"You can stay with me as long as you need to, you know that."

"Yeah, I know. But it might be easier for everybody if I just go to Mom's. Okay, listen, I'm gonna go. I'll see you when you get home. We're gonna head over to your place now."

"All right. I'll be there in thirty minutes or so. We're leaving the restaurant soon."

Olivia waited outside the ladies' room for a few moments after disconnecting the call. She still felt shaky and wanted to compose herself before going out and possibly being observed by Catherine Elliott. The last thing she needed was for Vivienne to find out that Thea had been at Stella's apartment when the fire broke out. Even though nothing that had happened was Stella's or Olivia's fault, Olivia could only imagine the spin Vivienne would put on the night's events.

But as she headed back toward the dining room, she saw Austin approaching, so she didn't have to see the Elliotts again.

"I got worried," he said. "Are you all right?"

"I'm okay. Have you paid the bill?"

"Yes."

"I'll tell you about the phone call once we're in the car. I need to get home quickly."

He looked as if he wanted to say something else, but he didn't. He simply took her arm and walked outside with her. A few minutes later, the valet parking attendant brought Austin's car around. Two minutes later, they were on their way back to Crandall Lake.

"I don't think you have to worry," Austin said when she'd told him what Stella had said. "Your mother-in-law won't know about Thea being there unless you tell her."

"Don't be so sure about that," Olivia said. "One of the firemen could be someone she knows. Or a bystander might have recognized Thea. Don't forget, Vivienne is very well-known."

"Well, even if she did find out, she certainly can't fault you for the fire. And your sister kept her wits about her, made sure Thea got out safely."

But no matter what Austin said, Olivia couldn't help worrying. Somehow Vivienne *always* heard the things you didn't want her to. And Olivia was sure, if she *did* find out about the fire, she'd find a way to use it against Olivia in the custody suit. Bottom line, tonight's events would be one more incident to show that Olivia didn't keep a close enough eye on Thea or make good judgment calls when it came to her welfare.

When they arrived at Olivia's house, Austin asked if he could come in. "I'd like to talk to your sister. Make sure I have all the facts straight."

"Of course."

Stella must have been watching for them, because she opened the front door before Olivia could use her key.

"Thea's in bed, but she's waiting for you to say good-night," Stella said.

"I'll go up. Austin wants to talk to you."

"Okay."

When Olivia reached Thea's room, Thea said, "Mommy, Mommy, did Aunt Stella tell you about the fire? I was carried down the ladder by a fireman!"

"Yes, honey, I know."

"It was 'citing. Just like a story!"

"Really? Exciting? Not scary?"

"No, Mommy, I wasn't scared." Thea's eyes shone. She loved drama. "And guess what? I was on television!" Olivia froze. Television? Oh, God. Now Vivienne was sure to find out about tonight. But she managed to tamp down her dismay and listen to Thea's account, then give her daughter a hug and good-night kiss before making her escape.

Austin and Stella were standing in the living room, talking. He turned at Olivia's entrance. "Brace yourself. A television crew was at the apartment, and they filmed Thea being rescued."

"Yes," Olivia said, sighing. "I know. Thea told me. She's all excited about it and probably won't fall asleep for hours."

"I'm sorry, Olivia," Stella said. "I didn't want to tell you over the phone. I knew you'd freak out."

Olivia sighed unhappily. "I can't help but think how Vivienne will just have one more thing to use against me now."

"If you hear anything from your in-laws—" Austin began.

"They won't call me," Olivia said, interrupting him. "I haven't heard directly from either one of them since this whole thing began. Actually, not since the day at the festival when Vivienne took Thea home with her."

"Good. You shouldn't be talking to them, anyway. All exchanges should be through me and their attorney."

"I'm so sorry about this," Stella said.

"It's not your fault," Austin said. Then he turned back to Olivia. "Please don't worry about this. I promise you, I'll take care of it. In fact, maybe I'll jump the gun and call Jackson Moyer myself. In the meantime, I'll be going. I know you're probably exhausted after this. I'll call you tomorrow."

"Okay." Olivia thought about the trip to San Antonio planned with Matt for tomorrow. Should she still go? Or should she stay home and figure out some kind of damage control? Maybe she should call Matt now. Let him know what had happened and see what he thought. She dreaded doing so, though, because she'd have to tell him she was out with Austin, and then he'd wonder why she hadn't told him where she was going to begin with.

Still debating what to do, Olivia, along with Stella, headed back upstairs to make sure Thea was settled down after Austin had gone. Surprisingly, she was half-asleep when they entered her room. Stella offered to read her a bedtime story, and when Thea agreed, Olivia thankfully left the two of them and went into her own bedroom to change into comfortable sweats. While there, she turned on the small television set mounted on her wall because it was almost time for the local news. She had decided to call Matt, but wanted to see what, if anything, was said about the fire before she did.

Her heart sank when she saw it was the lead story, and almost the first image was that of Thea being carried down the ladder from the third-floor balcony. She couldn't help feeling proud of her daughter, who didn't look frightened at all. But along with the pride was a huge dose of fear.

And the awful suspicion that Vivienne might have just been dealt a winning hand.

"Hugh! Hugh! Come and see this!" Vivienne had just settled down into her favorite chair in the sitting room off her bedroom, a glass of her favorite Bordeaux in her hand, and had switched on the local news at ten.

"What is so all-fired important?" her husband said irritably as he entered the room. "I was changing clothes."

"Look! Thea is on the news!"

"What?"

Vivienne even forgot about her wine—a nightly treat before bed—when she realized what the lead story was about. She was partly appalled and partly triumphant. Now everyone would see that she, Vivienne, was not being cruel or unreasonable to ask for custody of that precious child. How could they? Thea had been left at the apartment of that woman's sister, and look what had happened. Who knew who lived in those apartments? That was a totally unsuitable environment for Vivienne's granddaughter. And why was she there anyway? The child should be in bed no later than eight, and Vivienne would bet it was later than that when this all happened. Where was Olivia?

Vivienne bristled with indignation as she avidly watched the newscast. But she couldn't help swelling with pride over how her granddaughter showed absolutely no fear. Well, Vivienne certainly wasn't surprised about *that*. Good genes would always win out in the end. Thea's mother and her family might not possess the best lineage, but Thea's father and her paternal grandparents certainly did, and that was what was apparent now. That old saying about cream rising to the top had once again proven to be true.

"Well, I'll be damned," Hugh said when the segment was over and the newscasters had moved on to the next story.

All Vivienne did was smile. "This incident makes our case even stronger, you know." She finally picked up her wine and took a satisfying swallow. Her mind was spinning. Should she call and check on Thea? Was the child even home now? She wanted to call. She wanted to demand to speak to her granddaughter. She particularly wanted to tell that woman what she thought of her and her irresponsible behavior. But no matter how much she wanted to, she simply couldn't. Jackson Moyer had emphatically instructed them not to contact Thea or her mother directly.

From now on, every communication with or about your granddaughter needs to go through me, he'd said. *Don't forget that or you could jeopardize your chances of winning.*

Although Vivienne understood why he'd given them the directive, she couldn't help chafing under the rule because it wasn't in her nature to let others fight her battles. In fact, she relished the battles. They made her feel stronger and superior to her foes because she was powerful and intimidating, and she knew it, and she could almost always cow an adversary.

"I'm just glad Thea is all right," Hugh said now.

"Of course we're glad she's all right, but surely you see that what has happened is to our advantage."

Hugh sighed. "If you say so."

Vivienne's eyes narrowed. She was so tired of her mealymouthed husband's wishy-washy attitude about everything. For about the thousandth time she wondered what he'd say if he knew the truth. Sometimes she really wanted to tell him. To throw it in his face and see his expression. Would *that* finally get a rise out of him? Make him act like a man? Make her respect him, at least a little? But of course, her better judgment always won out and she kept silent. Her secret would remain her secret because that was in her best interest.

As Hugh walked back into their bedroom to resume changing into his pajamas, she made a decision. She might not be able to call and talk to Thea, but she would call Jackson Moyer tomorrow and make damned sure he knew all about the fire.

She was smiling as she settled back to finish her drink.

Chapter Twelve

Matt didn't see the news, but one of his buddies called him at ten fifteen to tell him about it. After they'd hung up, Matt immediately phoned Olivia.

"Hi, Matt." She sounded tired. "I was just thinking about calling you."

"Nolan Underwood called me and told me about the fire. Were you there? Was that Stella's apartment? Is Thea okay?"

"I wasn't there. Stella was babysitting. And Thea is fine. She considered the whole thing quite the adventure. She told me it was "citing." She loved being carried down the ladder."

He grinned. Sounded like Thea. "That's a relief."

"Yes. I was really upset when Stella called me. I'm sure your mother will have a field day over this."

"I'm afraid you're right. Most people would just be glad all's well that ends well, but she'll find a way to blame you even though you weren't there and the fire wasn't Stella's fault, at least according to what Nolan told me."

"No, it wasn't her fault. It started in an apartment below her. Unfortunately, though, her apartment received lots of damage, so she's going to be staying with my mother for a while. Thank goodness she bought rental insurance, so at least the damages will be covered."

"She was smart to do that."

"I actually think she was required to. Um, Matt… there's something I—"

"You're not going to tell me you don't want to go to San Antonio tomorrow?"

"No, I thought about it, but I really don't see any reason why we can't still go. I mean, Thea's fine. But there is something I need to tell you."

He didn't like the tone of her voice.

"I—I was out with Austin Crenshaw last night. We had a dinner meeting. At Hugo's. I should have told you that's where I was going when you asked me about spending the day with me. I don't know why I didn't. I mean, it really was just a meeting. Not a date."

Hugo's? Not a date? For a moment, Matt was flummoxed and couldn't think how to respond. Of course it was a date! Maybe Olivia wanted to believe otherwise, but Matt was sure Austin Crenshaw thought so. No man would take a woman to Hugo's for a dinner meeting. The place, not to mention the prices, literally screamed romance. Besides, Austin hadn't exactly made a secret of his interest in Olivia. "I see," he finally said.

The silence between them seemed to stretch forever.

When she broke it, her voice was pleading. "Come on, Matt…don't be like that."

"Like what?"

"You know like what. You're angry."

"I'm not angry. I'm just…confused, I guess. Hell, I thought after the other night things had changed. I thought we had an understanding."

"We do."

"Yet you had plans to go out with Austin Crenshaw and you didn't mention it when we talked. All you said was you had *a commitment*."

"It *was* a commitment, for a meeting. It wasn't a date."

"If it wasn't a date, you would have told me up front what you were doing. You would have simply said you were meeting with Austin to discuss the case."

When she didn't answer immediately, Matt knew he was right. She'd felt awkward and guilty. That's why she hadn't told him the truth. She'd known going out to dinner on a Saturday night couldn't be anything else *but* a date.

Maybe he was kidding himself. Maybe she didn't feel the same way about him that he felt about her. Maybe she regretted making love the other night and why she hadn't said she loved him, too. Maybe *that's* why she kept coming up with all kinds of excuses about why they couldn't be aboveboard about their relationship. Maybe it didn't have a damn thing to do with his mother.

He had to know. "Are you sorry about the other night?"

"Matt…"

"Just tell me, Olivia. I need to know the truth."

Seconds went by before she answered in a tired voice. "You know, Matt, it's late and I'm exhausted. Let's talk about this tomorrow."

"Thea will be with us tomorrow."

"So, what, then? Do you want to cancel tomorrow?"
He swallowed. "Do you?"

"No, Matt, I don't. But I don't see the point in going round and round on this subject. I'm not sorry about the other night with you and I've told you I don't consider tonight's meeting with Austin a date. And I've apologized for not immediately telling you about it. But you don't seem satisfied, so I don't know what else I can do."

Part of him—the hurt part of him—wanted to say it might be best to have a cooling-off period before seeing each other again, but the other part of him—the part that knew they were at some kind of crisis point in their relationship and that the next few minutes might determine which direction their future would take—told him maybe he was being unreasonable because he was jealous. Maybe, if he was smart, he needed to just swallow his pride.

"You're right," he said, softening his voice. "I accept your apology and think we should just forget about the whole thing. How about I'll pick you and Thea up around ten tomorrow morning?"

"We'll be ready. Good night, Matt."

"Good night, Olivia. I love you."

"I love you, too." This was said so softly, he wasn't sure he'd actually heard it or maybe imagined it because he'd wanted to hear it.

Sunday morning dawned clear and bright, with temperatures in the sixties and the promise of a beautiful day ahead. Unfortunately, Olivia awoke with a headache because she hadn't slept well. It had taken her hours to fall asleep, and then even after she had, she awakened several times in the night, disturbed by tumultuous dreams.

If only she hadn't gone out last night. It had been a really stupid thing to do, all the way around. She should have simply told Austin she'd come to his office in the morning or that she'd meet him somewhere for coffee during the day. Why hadn't she?

She put on her robe, then went downstairs, took some Advil and quietly fixed her morning coffee. Grateful Thea was still asleep, she padded barefoot into the living room and curled onto the sofa.

As she drank her coffee, her thoughts returned to last night and her phone conversation with Matt. In a way, she understood why he'd reacted as he had when she'd told him she'd been out with Austin. But in another way, his reaction still bothered her. Because either Matt trusted her or he didn't. Was it possible that his mother's constant undermining of her had planted seeds of doubt about her in Matt's subconscious? Seeds he didn't even know were there? Seeds that would grow into a kind of poison that would eventually ruin whatever chance they had?

By the time she'd finished her coffee and began to get ready for the day, she decided the time she and Thea and Matt spent together in San Antonio today would be a test. It would give her a clearer picture of how things really stood between them. If Matt seemed back to normal, then she'd do her best to forget about their conversation last night, too. But if he still seemed suspicious of her relationship with Austin or made any comments to that effect, then maybe she'd been right all along, and Matt had no place in her future.

Just the thought made her feel sick to her stomach. But yesterday's events had only brought back all her old doubts. Yes, she knew Matt loved her. And she loved him. Sometimes she ached from loving him and wanting him.

But was love…and desire…enough?

Could she bear being married to Matt when his mother despised her? Was a life filled with constant tension what she wanted for Thea? For herself?

Could she live that way?

Today, she needed to find some answers.

Even if she didn't like what she discovered.

Matt hadn't slept well, either.

He was sorry he'd implied he didn't believe Olivia. It wasn't her fault Austin was pursuing her. And the fact he was her attorney didn't make things easy for her. Instead of Matt piling more stress on her shoulders by criticizing her or inferring he didn't trust her, he should be a better man and totally support her. He *was* a better man. The problem was, he cared too much, and deep down he was afraid Olivia would never fully commit to him.

And realistically, why would she?

Family was of primary importance to her. She was a warm, giving, loving, generous person. Why would she want to remarry into a family headed by his mother? His mother had never given Olivia anything but heartache and grief, and all indications were that this kind of behavior would not only continue into the future, it would worsen.

Matt needed to do something to change this dynamic. But what? Everything he'd tried—talking to his mother, talking to his father, nothing had worked. If only he had something new, some way to persuade and influence his mother.

He was still thinking along these lines when he arrived at Olivia's home a few minutes before ten. But he purposely pushed all thoughts of his mother and his family situation out of his mind when he rang the doorbell. He wanted to give Olivia and Thea a wonderful carefree day, and he would not let his mother and her poison mar it. Later, at home alone again, would be time enough to go back to the problem.

When Olivia opened the door, an excited Thea at her side, love swept through him. He wanted nothing more than to gather both of them into his arms. But with Thea there and possible nosy neighbors, all he could do was smile down at the two females he loved most in the world. "Ready for our adventure?"

"Yes, Unca Matt!" Thea shouted. Then, practically jumping up and down, she said, "Did you see me on television?"

"No, sweetheart, I didn't. But I heard you were really brave."

"I was! And there were 'porters there!" Thea frowned. "But I didn't talk to them."

"'Porters?" Matt said.

"Reporters," Olivia said. "She wanted to talk to them. You know how she likes being in the spotlight," she added sotto voce.

"Maybe she'll be a performer of some sort when she grows up."

Olivia raised her eyebrows. "Don't encourage her."

"I am gonna be a 'porter when I'm big," Thea said, giving her mother a dark look.

Matt laughed. He couldn't help it. Thea was a handful now, at four. He couldn't imagine what she'd be like at fourteen. And at twenty-four. But he knew he wanted to be around to find out. And not just be around. He wanted these two people to be an intimate part of his life. He wanted Olivia as his wife and Thea as his child. And he also wanted more children, brothers and sisters, for Thea.

"How's that kitten of yours doing?" he said. "Did she see you on television last night?"

Now Thea's frown intensified. "Mommy said Kitty Kat has to stay in the laundry room while we're gone today."

"That seems sensible."

"Mommy's being mean," Thea said.

Olivia's eyes met Matt's. "I'm not being mean, Thea. Cats don't like traveling in cars, so we can't take Kitty Kat with us."

"I could hold her!" Thea insisted.

"Kitty Kat will be just fine at home," Olivia said patiently. "She's got her litter box, her food, her water. And she has that nice bed we bought for her."

"She'll be lonesome," Thea said, not appeased.

"Kittens don't get lonesome," Matt said. "She'll probably sleep away the whole day."

"If we don't get going, we won't have enough time in San Antonio," Olivia said, obviously wanting to take Thea's mind in a happier direction.

Her ploy worked. Thea immediately lost her frown. And five minutes later they were all in Matt's car and on their way.

The day turned out to be everything Matt had hoped it would be. They got to San Antonio well before noon, and since none of them were very hungry yet, they decided to take the riverboat tour first. Thea loved it and even Olivia seemed to completely relax and be more like her old self. One older woman said in an aside to Matt, "Your wife and daughter are lovely."

Matt didn't correct her. He simply smiled and said, "I think so, too."

At one o'clock they chose one of the riverside Mexican restaurants and snagged an outdoor table. Thea happily dove into the chips and salsa and, later, into the bowl of queso Matt ordered. Matt and Olivia allowed themselves one margarita each, they enjoyed the excellent food and watching the boats filled with tourists go by, and he felt the day was already a success.

After lunch they walked for a while, then headed for the market where Olivia bought Thea a bright red, embroidered Mexican dress and, for herself, a beautiful woven shawl in shades of blue. Matt bought both of them silver bangle bracelets, and Thea could hardly contain her excitement.

"Mine's just like yours, Mommy!" she kept saying while waving her arm in the air.

"I know, honey," Olivia said. "I love mine, too."

At that moment, with Thea between them, when Olivia's eyes met his, Matt knew he'd never been happier. If only he could stop the moment in time.

Then, on the way out of the market, Thea spied a handmade doll dressed in authentic Mexican costume, and Matt bought that for her, too. At first, Olivia objected, saying it was too expensive and Thea had to learn she couldn't have everything she wanted.

"It's an early Christmas present," Matt said.

"Please, Mommy," Thea begged.

"Please, Mommy," Matt said, smiling.

"Well…okay," Olivia said, relenting.

Thea fell asleep on the way home, and Matt and Olivia finally had a chance to talk about what was in the back of each of their minds.

Olivia introduced the subject after glancing behind

her to make sure Thea was asleep. "Have you forgiven me for yesterday?"

"You're the one who needs to do the forgiving," Matt said. "I shouldn't have reacted the way I did. Actually, I guess *overreacted* is the right word." Before she could say anything, he rushed ahead. He needed to make sure she understood. "I can't tell you how sorry I am, because I don't want you having doubts about us. The times I've told you that you and Thea are more important to me than anything else in my life, I've meant it. That will never change, and I want you to always remember that."

"I will."

He waited, but when she didn't echo his sentiment, he quickly realized she couldn't and tried not to let the omission bother him. Because of his mother, the looming custody case was probably the most important thing to Olivia right now, that and making sure Thea remained in her care. Her feelings for him had to be put on the back burner.

They fell silent for a while, and then Olivia said, "I hope we get word about the custody hearing soon."

"I imagine you will now that CPS has conducted their inspection. I wouldn't be surprised if you got notice tomorrow. If you don't, I'm sure Austin will check into it for you." He wanted to say he'd call Austin and make sure he did, but wisely kept that thought to himself.

A few minutes later, Olivia asked him about his campaign, and Matt belatedly realized he hadn't told her about his decision not to run. So for the rest of the trip home they discussed his promised appointment to temporary district attorney and the possibility of winning that position legitimately later on.

"Are you sure this is what you want, Matt? Your decision…it doesn't have anything to do with me, does it?"

"It is exactly what I want. The minute Carter made the suggestion, I knew it was perfect for me…and for us. So yes, every decision I make has something to do with you. And Thea."

She didn't say anything for long seconds. And when she did, her voice seemed flat. "What does your mother think about all this?"

"I only told her I wasn't running for the Senate. I didn't tell her about the DA's job."

"Why not?"

"Knowing her, she'd try to throw a monkey wrench into the appointment. That's what she does when things don't go her way. She ruins everything she touches." He immediately wanted to take the words back, but it was too late. He could have kicked himself.

Olivia didn't answer, and when he glanced at her, he saw she was staring out her window. Why hadn't he simply said he would tell his parents when the time was right, and drop it at that? Why had he had to remind Olivia of everything she feared in a relationship with him?

Dammit! They were almost home, and this wasn't the way he wanted to end the day.

"Let's talk about something more pleasant," he said almost desperately. "Like ordering a pizza for dinner. Or we could get Chinese takeout."

"I'm not really very hungry after that big lunch," Olivia said. "I'm sorry, Matt, but I think Thea and I will just have soup or something light, and I'll go to bed when she does tonight. I didn't get much sleep last night and I'm on the day shift tomorrow."

Disappointment flooded him. Reality had once again reared its ugly head. Already, the fun-filled day of San

Antonio had been replaced with reminders of the custody suit and what would be in store for them in the coming days here at home.

He silently cursed his mother. Every single negative thing in their lives right now could be directly traced to her. Was there any way to stop her before she ruined their lives completely?

Chapter Thirteen

Olivia decided she would give her notice Monday morning. So as soon as she arrived at the hospital, she told Helena Tucker, her supervisor, that she needed to talk to her.

"Oh, Olivia, I hate to hear this," Helena said, dismay written all over her face. "You're one of the best people I've got on my team. I don't want to lose you."

Olivia sighed. "Thank you, I appreciate that, but something has happened that's made me think about the future sooner than I'd expected to." Although she had not told anyone other than her family about the custody suit, she decided it was only fair to tell Helena.

"Unbelievable," Helena said when she'd finished. "Why, you're one of the best mothers I know. Listen, Olivia, if you need a character witness, you can count on me."

Olivia was touched. She knew her boss liked her,

but she hadn't expected this kind of loyalty. "I can't tell you how much that means to me. I'll keep your offer in mind."

"Well, I'm serious. So don't hesitate to ask. Now, can I count on you to stay on until I can replace you?"

"As long as it doesn't drag on too long," Olivia said. "I'd like to be free after the holidays."

"Oh, that shouldn't be a problem. I'm pretty sure Shari wants to go full-time, and I also have a couple of applications hanging fire."

As Olivia turned to leave, Helena said, "We'll miss you around here."

"I'll miss you, too." But mixed with her regret over leaving a job she loved, Olivia also felt tremendous relief.

It would be wonderful not to have to worry about the days Thea was under the weather and Olivia had to prevail upon her mother to watch her. Besides, Olivia would enjoy being home with Thea, and once Thea started first grade and was gone most of the day, Olivia could follow through with her renewed desire to earn her nursing degree. So she felt excitement as well as regret. Of course, all her plans hinged on winning the custody case.

That damned case.

It loomed over everything. Some days she still had trouble believing her in-laws were actually doing this to her.

Despite the worry it caused, she managed to put the custody suit out of her mind as the busy morning progressed, but it came hurtling back when she got a phone call from Austin over her lunch hour.

"The hearing has been scheduled for this coming Friday afternoon," he said without preamble. "Our instructions are to be at family court at two o'clock."

Olivia swallowed. "Will…will we know right away?"

"I don't know. Depends on the judge. I checked the docket, and Judge Lawrence will be hearing the case."

"Do you know him?"

"It's not a him. Her name is Althea Lawrence, and she's been a judge in family court for almost twenty years. I'm told she's very good. Very fair. Very family friendly. She has four kids of her own."

Olivia closed her eyes. Before, even though she'd known all of this was actually happening, it had somehow seemed surreal. Now it felt totally real. And frightening. In just four days, her entire future would be determined by some woman she'd never met, a woman who would hear so-called "evidence" against her and then rebuttal witnesses who would attest to her good character and fitness as a mother, not to mention the unknown recommendation of Joan Barwood, the caseworker who had visited her.

"And Thea will be questioned?" she asked faintly.

"Probably. We've been instructed to bring someone along who can stay with Thea during the hearing, because they won't allow a child as young as she is to be present during testimony. She'll be in a room nearby especially set up for young children, and someone will need to be with her until she's called."

"She'll actually be called into the hearing itself? Be questioned in front of all of us?"

"I'm not sure. She might be interviewed in the judge's chambers. Or maybe the judge will go into the children's room and talk to her there."

"And we won't know what's being said?"

"We may see the interview on closed circuit television. It's up to the judge."

"Everyone in the court room?"

"No. I think just you and me, your in-laws and Jackson Moyer."

Olivia fought back tears. "I hate this."

"I know you do. I hate it for you. And for Thea. But take heart, Olivia. We have a really good case, and I think we'll win. Just keep your chin up and let the truth speak for itself."

Yes. And she'd also pray. She'd pray like she'd never prayed before.

"What do you think I should tell Thea? I mean, surely she needs to be prepared."

"I've talked to a buddy of mine who's handled a couple of these types of cases, and he tells me it's best to be honest with her. Explain that her grandparents think it would be best for her to live with them, but you want her to stay with you, and that because you disagree, a judge has been instructed to find out how Thea feels."

"What if she asks questions about her grandmother? Questions I don't feel comfortable answering?" Olivia thought about how just the other day Thea had wanted to take the new kitten and go and visit "Mimi" and Olivia had to put her daughter off.

"I know it's hard, but be careful what you say," Austin said. "The judge will probably ask Thea what you've told her, and it's best you don't criticize either grandparent."

Olivia couldn't help thinking this was all kind of like a nasty divorce where a mother who loved her child had to make sure not to let that child know there were any bad feelings.

They talked for a while longer, and then Austin got another call and said if she had more questions, he'd be available that evening and not to hesitate to call him.

But as reassuring as Austin had been, Matt was the one Olivia really wanted to talk to.

She decided to call him right away, but his secretary told her he was in court and wouldn't be back for several hours. "Shall I have him call you?"

"No," Olivia said, "I'm at work. But tell him I called and will call him tonight."

Then she went back to her department and explained to Helena she'd have to have Friday off, and why.

For the rest of the day, even though Olivia did her job thoroughly, she had a hard time thinking of anything else but what was in store for her at the end of the week.

Olivia dressed carefully for the hearing at family court. With her mother's and Stella's approval, she put on a simple dark green dress with a round neckline and slightly flared skirt that ended just below her knees. Sensible two-inch heeled pumps, a single strand of pearls and tiny pearl earrings completed her ensemble. She carefully applied her makeup: just a bit of foundation and a touch of eye shadow and mascara. A rosy lip gloss completed the picture. She thought she looked like exactly what she was: a young mother from a small town.

"Perfect," her mother declared. She hugged Olivia, saying, "Honey, it's all going to be okay."

"I hope so," Olivia said, swallowing her fear. But no matter how many times she reassured herself, she couldn't make her heart stop its too-fast rhythm. Even deep breathing didn't help.

I can't lose Thea. I can't.

She was so grateful Matt would be there today, even though she knew his mother would be furious when she saw him, obviously giving Olivia his support. He'd also told both her and Austin he was available to testify on her behalf. Olivia hoped that wouldn't be necessary because no good would come of his openly challenging his mother like that. And yet, how could she tell Matt to stay away? Especially if, as he believed, the judge would be swayed by his presence?

Olivia had been instructed to be outside the courtroom by one forty-five that afternoon, ready to be called when the judge returned from lunch. She hoped the scheduling meant that her case would be concluded by the day's end and not be carried over till the following week.

Austin was meeting them there. Olivia, Thea, Norma and Stella arrived a little after one thirty. When they walked into the courthouse, Olivia saw Matt and Austin standing talking. She also saw her in-laws, accompanied by a very tall, imposing man—whom Olivia assumed was the famous Jackson Moyer—at the other end of the hallway. Vivienne looked in her direction only once, then abruptly turned away. As always, the woman looked impeccable in a dark blue ensemble.

"There's Mimi!" Thea said, a big smile lighting her face. "Can we go see her, Mommy?"

"Not now, sweetie. Later, maybe," Olivia said, trying to keep her voice normal even though her stomach was churning. Matt turned at the sound of their voices, and their eyes met. In his, she saw encouragement and support. Instantly, she felt better.

He smiled at her, walked over and drew her into a hug, whispering, "It's going to be okay."

"Matt, your parents can see you," she said, pulling away even though, at that moment, what she wanted most in the world—aside from winning today's case— was the comfort of his arms.

"I don't care," he said. Then, shocking her, he said loud enough for her family and Austin to hear, "I love you, and I don't care who knows it."

Olivia didn't know where to look…or what to say. She could feel herself blushing. It was one thing for her family to suspect how things stood between her and Matt, quite another to state it so publicly.

Her mother touched her arm and smiled at her reassuringly. "We all love you, honey. Everything's going to be fine."

Olivia's eyes finally met Austin's. In them she saw resignation. But she also saw Austin's integrity, strength and determination. He would do his best for her, no matter what. He gave her an encouraging smile, then echoed her mother's sentiment. "It really is going to be fine, Olivia. I promise you."

She took a deep shaky breath.

And prayed everyone was right.

Matt sat in the very back of the courtroom, even though he wished he had the right to sit beside Olivia, to hold her hand, to show the world how much he believed in her. His mother had given him a cold stare as she'd walked in; his father had evaded Matt's gaze.

Matt was glad he'd been able to persuade his sister to stay away. There was no sense in her getting embroiled in this lunacy. If he'd thought Madeleine's support for Olivia would make a difference, he might have advised her to come despite his mother, but he didn't think it would, so it had seemed more prudent for Madeleine to stay out of the fray.

A few minutes after all interested parties had settled into their places, the door leading to the judge's chambers opened and the bailiff called, "All rise!" as Judge Althea Lawrence entered.

Once the judge was seated, Matt studied her. He'd boned up on her background and knew she was fifty-three, a plus because sometimes older judges tended to be more conservative. She came from a fairly large blue-collar family and had put herself through college and law school with a mix of scholarships, loans and part-time jobs. That background was also a plus. Odds were she'd be much more inclined to identify with Olivia than with Vivienne. And the final plus—she was a mother herself.

The judge greeted the participants, then read the petition aloud. When she'd finished, she said, "Mr. Moyer, as counsel for the petitioner, let's hear your first witness."

The first witness turned out to be Janice Rosen, the ER nurse who had attended when Olivia brought Thea in after the incident in the backyard where her lip had been cut. Jackson Moyer adroitly questioned the nurse in a way that made her answers seem as if the accident had been Olivia's fault because she hadn't been watching Thea the way she should have.

When Moyer finished, Austin rose.

"Do you have any children, Mrs. Rosen?" he asked, smiling at her in a friendly way.

"I do."

"And how old are they?"

"Five and seven."

"Boys or girls?"

"Two boys."

"I'll bet they can be a handful."

The nurse grinned. "Two handfuls."

Austin chuckled. "And I'll bet they can get into things in a second. Even when you're in the room."

"You can say that again. I've gotta have eyes in the back of my head."

"Have you ever left them playing outside while you ran into the house to get something?"

"Of course. Who hasn't?"

Austin nodded. "That's right. Who hasn't?" He looked at the judge as if to say, *And I'll bet you have, too. Because a parent can't be with a child every second. And even if they are, accidents will still happen, won't they?*

"Have one of your boys ever had an accident at home?" Austin said, turning his attention back to the nurse.

"Objection, Your Honor," Jackson Moyer said. "We aren't here to investigate Ms. Rosen's parenting skills."

"Sustained," the judge said. "Move on, Mr. Crenshaw."

"One last question, Mrs. Rosen," Austin said. "Did the attending physician note anything unusual about the circumstances of Thea Britton's accident that day? Did he feel it was caused by neglect? Recommend that CPS be called?"

"No. Nothing like that."

"Thank you. Nothing further."

Matt relaxed a bit after that. Austin obviously knew what he was doing. He'd made the witness comfortable, been friendly, and hadn't tried to intimidate her with his questions.

The next witness was Phyllis Grimm, who lived next door to Olivia's mother. She testified about an incident that had taken place on Thea's third birthday when Thea had darted toward the street. "Her mother's whole family were standing right there and nobody was holding that child's hand! She could have been killed."

Jackson Moyer nodded sagely when she'd finished. "Thank you, Mrs. Grimm," he said. "We appreciate your taking the time to come here today and tell us about this truly frightening incident."

Austin greeted Phyllis Grimm respectfully as he approached and echoed Jackson Moyer's thanks for her appearance in court. Then he said, "Isn't it true, Mrs. Grimm, that in addition to her mother's family, both of Thea's Britton grandparents were also present during the stated incident?"

Phyllis Grimm visibly stiffened in her seat. "I don't know who all was there. I just know it was a noisy party they were having and I happened to be looking out the window when I saw the little girl run into the street."

"A noisy party? But it was held inside, wasn't it?" Austin consulted his notes. "And the party was actually over, I believe. Mr. and Mrs. Britton were leaving and the others had walked outside to say goodbye to them."

The Grimm woman, whose sour look hadn't changed, shrugged. "Whatever."

Matt knew the woman had an ax to grind with Norma Dubrovnik because of a broken fence that separated their property. She had demanded that Norma replace the fence. Norma had tried to reason with her because the fence was on the dividing line of the property, and each owner traditionally paid half when the fence was a common one. The dispute had gone on for months now.

"Did you also see that Thea was chasing a baby rabbit? And that before she reached the street her mother ran after her and caught her and that no harm came to her?"

"No, I didn't," the woman said angrily. "Do you think

I spend all day looking out my window? I just know the mother wasn't watching her child properly."

"Your Honor," Austin said, "we will be calling a rebuttal witness later who will verify that Thea's mother was, indeed, watching her child and that Thea was caught before she ever went into the street." He then turned to Phyllis Grimm, saying, "No more questions for this witness."

The next witness was a young woman who testified she'd seen Thea falling off a swing at the park because Olivia's mother's attention was elsewhere.

"She got very upset, too," the woman said.

"Thea?"

"No, the older woman, the grandmother. She was so shook up I had to take care of the little girl myself. Luckily she wasn't hurt badly. Just a knee scrape."

"So the child's grandmother wasn't able to manage a child as lively as Thea Britton," Moyer said.

"Objection, Your Honor," Austin said. "Leading the witness."

"Sustained."

"Withdrawn, Your Honor." Moyer turned to Austin. "Your witness, Counselor."

Austin did his best, but he was unable to shake the woman's staunch belief that Norma Dubrovnik hadn't been capable of the kind of vigilance and energy necessary to provide adequate child care.

"The grandmother told me she felt dizzy herself," the woman insisted. "And now I've learned she's a diabetic! My sister's a diabetic, and I know how careful she has to be to eat the right things at the right time. I'll bet that was the problem. She was probably having low blood sugar."

Matt grimaced. Austin quickly protested that Norma's

diabetes had no bearing on the issue at hand, and the judge concurred, so Matt relaxed. Still, personally, he hated hearing anything negative about Olivia's mother, because she was a wonderful person. The last witness before Vivienne herself would appear was Officer Tom Nicholls. Matt was surprised. He'd expected a bystander or two from the festival; what he hadn't expected was one of the police officers.

Officer Nicholls spoke unemotionally, just gave the facts of what had happened at the festival when Thea disappeared. Without accusation, he admitted that dozens of officers were involved in the subsequent search, as well as many others not involved in law enforcement.

Jackson Moyer cleverly continued questioning him about specifics of that day and managed to elicit the information that the reason Olivia and her family had been distracted and not realized Thea had wandered off was because her grandmother Dubrovnik had collapsed from a diabetic blood sugar low.

As the afternoon wore on, Matt could see that Norma's condition was going to play a big part in his parents' case against Olivia and her judgment as a mother. He could only imagine what his mother would have to say when she had her turn to testify. Poor Norma. She was going to be the scapegoat here, and if Olivia lost custody of Thea, Norma would always feel guilty.

"But isn't it true, Officer Nicholls," Austin asked when it was his turn to question the man, "that the petitioner, Vivienne Britton, was ultimately the person responsible for Thea's disappearance from the festival? That if she hadn't interfered, or had at least notified Thea's mother, that she had found the child, none of the hundreds of people involved in the search would have been necessary?"

"That's one interpretation of what happened," the officer said, "but it's my understanding that Mrs. Britton— the elder Mrs. Britton—found Thea Britton wandering alone and took her home with her for safety reasons."

Matt's jaw hardened. Obviously, his parents—his mother, more exactly—had been at work here and influenced the officer's thinking.

It was almost five o'clock before Nicholls had finished testifying. Judge Lawrence looked at the clock, then said, "It's too late for more testimony today. We will resume hearing this case Monday morning at nine o'clock. All parties should plan to be here for most of the day."

Jackson Moyer and Matt's parents immediately stood and, without looking in Olivia's direction, walked out of the courtroom. Neither parent acknowledged Matt as they passed by.

"I think things went well," Matt said when he joined Olivia's group. His eyes sought Olivia's and he could see how exhausted she was. The strain of the proceedings had already taken a toll.

"I agree," Austin said. "We refuted every claim they made, and Monday, when our witnesses testify, it's going to make an even bigger difference."

Olivia tried to smile, but Matt could see how hard the afternoon had been for her. He knew the testimony about her mother had been difficult to hear. He was thankful Norma hadn't been in the courtroom herself and was actually surprised Jackson Moyer hadn't somehow been able to get that information in. Then he realized the disclosure would probably come when his mother got her day in court.

"Olivia looks tired," he said in an aside to Stella. "Did she drive here today?"

"No, she and Thea rode with me and Mom."

"Why don't you let me take her home?"

Stella smiled in understanding. "That's fine with me. I'll take Mom to dinner somewhere before we go back."

Olivia didn't protest when Matt told her the plan. When the two of them went to collect Thea, they found she'd fallen asleep. Norma herself sat quietly crocheting. She rose when they entered the room.

Olivia explained and she and her mother kissed goodbye. Norma smiled at Matt and he bent down and kissed her cheek before she left to join Stella. "Don't worry," he said quietly. "It'll go much better on Monday." Then he picked up Thea and, accompanied by Olivia, left the room.

As they walked out of the courthouse together, Matt saw his parents standing on the sidewalk in front, talking to Jackson Moyer.

"Matt…" Olivia said faintly.

"Don't look at them," he said. "Hold your head up high and keep walking."

She only hesitated a moment, then did as he'd instructed. His heart felt full to bursting.

He had never been prouder of her.

Chapter Fourteen

"Would you mind getting the mail for me?" Olivia asked after Matt had brought Thea into the house. Because she'd missed her nap, she hadn't awakened on the drive home and was even now sleeping soundly on the daybed in the study.

Olivia wondered what Matt had thought when he'd deposited her there. Was he remembering the Monday night they'd made love on that very same bed? She knew she was. Every time she looked at that bed she remembered that night.

"Sure," he said.

While Matt went outside to the mailbox, Olivia walked back to the kitchen to figure out what she would feed Thea for supper. Maybe it was a grilled cheese and tomato soup kind of night. Or maybe she'd call for Chinese takeout. Thea loved the honey-glazed shrimp that was a specialty of their favorite restaurant.

"Here you go," Matt said, walking into the kitchen. He handed her the mail: a bill from the water department, an L.L. Bean catalog, two other pieces of junk mail and a large Priority Mail envelope.

Olivia looked at the envelope curiously. The return address was that of a law firm in Austin. "What in the world?" she said, pulling at the tape that would open the envelope.

She stared at the letter that had been inside. As she read, her mouth fell open. The law firm—Standish, Davis, and Standish—were pleased to inform her that she and her daughter, Dorothea Lynn Britton, were the main heirs to the estate of the late Jonathan Pierce Kendrick, who had died the previous week. The estate was worth an estimated twelve million dollars. Olivia or her lawyer were instructed to call their law office as soon as possible for more information and details on claiming the estate. Stunned, Olivia handed the letter to Matt.

He read it quickly, then looked at her. He looked as bewildered as she felt. "Who is this Jonathan Kendrick?" he asked.

"I have no idea."

"Twelve million dollars?" he said softly. "And you don't know who he is?"

"No. I've never heard of him." Olivia frowned. "Could this be some kind of hoax? A scam, maybe?"

"No, I don't think so. Standish, Davis, and Standish is a well-known and very reputable Austin law firm. In fact, I know the younger Standish. Kenny and I went to law school together."

"It says to call them." Olivia looked at the clock. It was almost six o'clock. "Do you think they'd still be there?"

"Let me try," Matt said. He pulled his cell out of his

pocket. A moment later he said, "Yes, may I speak to Ken Standish? Tell him it's Matt Britton." He smiled at Olivia, mouthing, "We're in luck. He's still there."

Olivia sat down at the kitchen table and motioned for Matt to do so, too. She listened as he began to talk to Ken Standish, explaining that he was her brother-in-law and had been with her when she'd received their letter about Jonathan Kendrick's estate.

"Of course. I understand," Matt said. "Here. I'll let you talk to her yourself." He handed her his phone.

"Hello?" she said.

"Hello, Mrs. Britton. This is Kenneth Standish. I'm guessing you're shocked by our letter."

"That's a good description. I can't really wrap my head around what you said. I mean, why would a perfect stranger leave me and my daughter so much money?"

"Yes, well, I can understand your confusion. Look, Mrs. Britton, I'd love to explain everything to you now, but I don't think it's a good idea to discuss this over the phone. Or in the presence of your brother-in-law."

"But…why not? I don't understand."

"I know you don't. But it would just be better if you and your attorney come to my office Monday morning. Wait. Is Matt your attorney?"

Olivia swallowed. Looked at Matt. He was frowning. "Um, no. Not really."

"Good. I think it's best your attorney is a neutral party."

A neutral party?

"Um, I actually do have an attorney. Austin Crenshaw."

"Really? I know Austin. For something like this, he's a great choice. I'll give him a call. Set up something for Monday."

"Monday won't work, Mr. Standish. I have to be in court in San Marcos on Monday. Which is actually why I have an attorney."

Ken Standish was silent for a moment. Then he said, "What about tomorrow? Would that work?"

Olivia wet her lips. "Yes. That would work."

"Okay, I'll call Austin and he'll call you and let you know what time. I'm looking forward to meeting you."

"M-me, too," Olivia said.

"Well?" Matt said when she disconnected the call.

"He...wouldn't tell me anything. He said I should bring my attorney and come to his office and then he'd explain. He...he said it would be best not to say anything over the phone."

Matt's frown intensified. "I don't understand this."

"I don't, either." *A neutral party.* What had Standish meant?

"I think I should go with you tomorrow."

"Um, Mr. Standish said just to bring Austin."

Now Matt's expression turned to bewilderment. "What? No one else can come? Not even me?"

Since Olivia couldn't say "particularly not you," she simply said, "He stressed that I should only bring my attorney."

"But Olivia, I don't—" He broke off whatever else he'd meant to say because at that moment, Thea walked into the room. She was rubbing her eyes and yawning.

"Hey, sweetheart," Matt said, smiling down at her. "Did you have a good nap?"

"I'm hungry, Mommy," Thea said.

Olivia knew, just from the tone of Thea's voice, that she was cranky and would remain out of sorts until Olivia managed to get her in bed for the night. "How about some tomato soup and grilled cheese?"

"I want a chocolate milk shake!" Her lower lip protruded.

A tantrum seemed imminent. "I can do chocolate milk. But I don't have any ice cream to make a milk shake," Olivia said in her most persuasive voice.

The look on Thea's face would have been comical if the atmosphere hadn't already been so tense. When thwarted, Thea could be impossible. "I want a milk shake!" she shouted. For good measure, she stamped her foot.

Olivia's eyes met Matt's. "Sorry," she said, preparing herself for the coming full-fledged thunderstorm.

"Why don't I run over to the store and pick up some Blue Bell?" Matt said. He gave Thea an even bigger smile. "Then you can have your milk shake."

Thea looked at him, her face a road map of her thoughts.

"Would you?" Olivia said gratefully. She knew she shouldn't give in to Thea, but she was too worn out to be the perfect parent tonight.

By the time Matt returned, Thea was settled into her booster chair and more or less happily eating a grilled cheese sandwich, accompanied by a big daub of ketchup—she'd passed on the tomato soup—and Olivia was tiredly drinking a glass of wine while trying not to think about the tense day in court or the shocking news she'd received less than an hour ago or who Jonathan Kendrick was or why Ken Standish had not wanted Matt to accompany her tomorrow.

"Thank you," she said to Matt, getting up and putting the ice cream in the freezer until Thea was finished with the sandwich. "Would you like a grilled cheese sandwich, too?"

"I'm not hungry," he said. His eyes were troubled. "When do you think she'll be ready for bed?"

He wants to continue our earlier discussion. "I think she's ready now, but getting her there will be a problem."

"How about if I help and after she's down we can talk?"

Olivia fought her exhaustion. None of the stress she felt was Matt's fault. She had to remember that. "Matt, please don't take this the wrong way, but I'm so tired. I just want to go to bed myself. And really, what is there to talk about?" She dropped her voice to almost a whisper, even though Thea didn't seem to be paying any attention to them. "I don't want to talk about the custody hearing and there's nothing more to say about that letter until after I meet with Mr. Standish tomorrow."

"So you want me to leave?"

He's hurt. "Please don't be mad. I promise I'll tell you everything after tomorrow's meeting."

His shoulders slumped. "I'm not mad. I'm disappointed."

"In *me*?"

"I guess I thought you'd take me to that meeting. That you'd want *me* to be your attorney."

For just a moment, Olivia considered an evasion. But if they couldn't be truthful with each other, how could there ever be real trust between them? Their relationship would be doomed regardless of the outcome of the custody suit. "Mr. Standish said it was better if my attorney was a neutral party."

Matt's face revealed his shock. "And he was referring to *me*? What does *that* mean?"

"I don't know, Matt. I'm just telling you what he said."

"But, Olivia, that doesn't make any sense. Don't *you* want me to be there?"

"Of course, I want you to be there, but—"

Thea chose that moment to bang on the table and demand her milk shake. "I've got to tend to Thea, Matt." Exhaustion caused her to sound impatient, but suddenly the stress of the past weeks just seemed to pile in on her. "Can we table this discussion until after my meeting tomorrow? Hopefully, that'll shed light on everything."

Matt wasn't happy; that much was obvious, but he didn't argue. Instead, he just dropped a light kiss on her mouth, said, "Let me know what time you're going tomorrow, and get a good night's sleep. And remember… I love you."

"I love you, too," she murmured.

"Mommy!" Thea yelled.

"One milk shake coming up," Olivia said, forcing herself to move, even though all she really wanted was to sink down into one of the kitchen chairs and bury her face in her arms. But she was a mother, first and foremost. So she sighed and opened the freezer door. As she took the ice cream out, she heard the front door open and shut.

Matt was gone.

And tomorrow couldn't come soon enough.

Austin and Olivia were ushered into Ken Standish's office at ten o'clock Saturday morning. Olivia felt better than she had the night before, although her stomach was still tied up in knots because she hated the way she and Matt had parted. On top of that, she still couldn't wrap her head around the fact that some man she'd never heard of before had left her and her daughter an estimated twelve million dollars. In fact, even though she and Austin were in Ken Standish's office, nothing about why they were there seemed real.

"I'll get right to the point," Standish said after inviting Olivia and Austin to be seated and offering them something to drink.

He was a pleasant-faced man with a warm smile. Olivia liked him immediately.

"I know you're wondering why Jonathan Pierce Kendrick named you and your daughter his heirs," he continued.

"Especially since I've never even heard of him," Olivia said.

"The reason for that is, while he was alive, he chose to keep his identity secret. But he always intended that after his death the truth would be revealed."

"What truth?" Austin asked.

Standish looked at Olivia. "Jonathan Kendrick was your late husband's birth father. And your daughter's grandfather."

"What! But—" She stared at the lawyer. How was this possible? Could it be true?

Standish nodded. "I know. It's hard to believe. But it's true. And it can easily be proven by testing your daughter's DNA. Mr. Kendrick had his DNA documented many years ago in anticipation of this day."

Olivia sat there, stunned. Had Vivienne known this? Did Hugh? Did *Matt*? Is that why Standish had suggested Matt might not be a neutral party?

"My God, Olivia," Austin said. "Do you know what this means? There's no way your in-laws will win the custody case now."

"Custody case?" Standish said, frowning.

"Yes. The elder Brittons are petitioning the court for custody of Thea, Olivia's daughter," Austin explained.

"On what grounds?"

"That Olivia is an unfit mother. The charges are ridiculous, of course, but the court won't just take our word for it now that an accusation has been made. CPS was notified and has conducted an investigation. We'll be hearing their recommendations on Monday."

Standish turned to Olivia. "I'm very sorry to hear this. If I can help in any way, I'll be happy to. Um…" He cleared his throat. "Mr. Kendrick had you thoroughly investigated, himself, both initially, when you married your husband, and periodically over the years. In that way, he always looked after your daughter. So Austin is right. You've got perfect leverage now. Not just the fact that Hugh Britton is not your daughter's grandfather, but everything documented in Jonathan Kendrick's files."

"But even if this is all true, maybe my father-in-law knows all about it," Olivia said.

"He doesn't," Standish said. "Mr. Kendrick's papers explain exactly why he kept his identity secret. It was to protect your mother-in-law. He wrote you a letter, Olivia. Why don't we give you some privacy and you can read it, and after you read it, we can talk more. In the meantime, I'll explain to Austin what steps will need to be taken for you to claim the estate."

Before he and Austin left his office for a nearby conference room, he handed Olivia an envelope. Olivia's hands were shaking when she opened it.

Dear Olivia,
You don't know me, but I know a lot about you. I've kept track of you for many years—you and your beautiful daughter, my granddaughter—my only grandchild, in fact. After Mark died, you and she were the two reasons my life still had mean-

ing, because I have never been blessed with other children. I've often regretted my promise to Vivienne to keep my identity a secret, especially since Mark's death. I understood her reasons for silence and respected them. I loved her—we were once engaged, you see, before she met Hugh Britton and broke our engagement—and we reconnected, briefly, during a rough patch in their marriage. That's when Mark was conceived. Neither of us knew it until after she and Hugh had reconciled, and by then, she wasn't willing to leave him.

I kept my promise of silence for a long time. But now that I'm facing my own mortality, I think I made a mistake. All these years, you and I and Thea could have known one another, and I could have perhaps made your life easier. I'm sorry I didn't come forward sooner, but I hope that doing so now will make a positive difference in your life. If others are hurt by this disclosure, I'm sorry, but the truth needs to be told, for many reasons.

I admire you and respect you and think you are a wonderful mother. Please tell my granddaughter how much I love her and how proud I am to know I am responsible for some of her genes.

With much love,

Jonathan P. Kendrick

Olivia's eyes were moist when she finished reading the letter. He sounded like such a lovely man. How she wished she'd known about him sooner. And yet, she couldn't help feeling bad for Hugh. Did he have any idea Vivienne had been unfaithful to him? That Mark was not his son?

And Matt.

Did Matt know? Suspect? She didn't believe he did; he would have told her if he had. Especially since he'd freely admitted to her how much his mother had favored Mark. Even Mark had told her about Vivienne's favoritism and how uncomfortable it had made him, because Mark had loved and respected Matt. The brothers had been close, despite Vivienne's adulation of her youngest son.

And now Olivia knew why that adulation had existed. Vivienne must have still loved Jonathan Kendrick, even though she chose to stay in her marriage. Olivia could almost feel sorry for Vivienne. Almost. But nothing excused the unhappiness Vivienne had caused in other people's lives. It especially didn't excuse her recent behavior.

Still…no matter how or why Vivienne had become the person she now was, Olivia didn't want to be the one responsible for exposing her sins to the world. After all, she was *still* Thea's grandmother. Still Mark's mother. And still Matt's mother. And even if Olivia were willing to face off with Vivienne, the truth might destroy Hugh.

I can't do that to them.

Olivia was still thinking about the letter and its ramifications when Austin and Ken Standish came back into the office.

"I've made a decision," she said.

Both men looked at her.

"I don't want to use what we've learned today as a weapon against my mother-in-law."

"But, Olivia—" Austin said.

"No." Olivia shook her head. "I won't be persuaded otherwise. You said yourself we have a strong case. I don't want to expose her. I don't want to hurt Hugh… or the rest of the family."

"We do have a strong case, and actually, I received a phone call from the investigator I hired to look into all of Vivienne's so-called evidence while Ken and I were giving you privacy to read your letter, and he's turned up something potentially very good for our case. But you could still lose. There's no telling how the judge will rule. And once a ruling is made, it will be very difficult to change."

Olivia shook her head. "You can't use the information about Mark's paternity. I won't allow it." Making this public would ruin Vivienne. It would ruin Hugh. And it would completely ruin any chance of any kind of reconciliation with the family. "When Thea's older, she'll have to be told the truth, but not now. Not like this. No matter what she's done, I won't destroy Vivienne's reputation."

"Olivia, be sensible. They are trying to destroy *yours*. They're lying about you, using any means at their disposal to try to take your daughter away from you. You have to fight back."

"I will fight back, but not that way. I can't. Tell me what our investigator found."

Austin sighed. "Vivienne is the reason Thea wandered off during the festival. I know we all thought it was a kitten or some other animal that drew her attention, but it wasn't. Our investigator found out Vivienne did it on purpose, just to make you look bad."

"How could the investigator possibly know that?"

"Because she was seen doing it. He has a sworn eyewitness statement."

Olivia was stunned. Did Matt know his mother was behind Thea's disappearance? She remembered the way he'd called his family after finding out Thea was missing. How he told her he hoped the custody case could be settled without dragging all of them through the mud. He must have, at least, suspected.

And he'd never said anything.

But almost immediately after thinking all this, she was ashamed of herself. How could she doubt Matt, even for one second? He couldn't have known. Not Matt.

He would have told her.

Chapter Fifteen

Matt couldn't concentrate on anything Saturday morning. He went into the office to catch up on paperwork, but he accomplished very little. He kept waiting for his phone to ring, willing each call to be from Olivia. When, at one o'clock, she still hadn't called, he finally texted her.

Austin will call you, she texted back.

Austin? Why couldn't *she* call him? What the hell was going on?

Twenty minutes later, Austin called.

Matt listened without interrupting as Austin told him what they'd learned in Ken Standish's office and then what his investigator had turned up concerning Thea's disappearance from the Fall Festival.

"I'm frustrated, because Olivia has forbidden me to use the information about your brother's paternity, which, on top of what the investigator found, would ensure she'd keep custody of Thea."

Matt wasn't shocked by the information about his mother luring Thea from the festival—it was exactly the kind of thing she *would* do and he was surprised he hadn't suspected her.

Nor was he really shocked about Mark. He'd always known Mark was the favorite of his mother's children, and now he finally understood why. He'd also known about the problems in his parents' marriage. They'd been evident from the time he was old enough to understand. But he had always imagined his father might be the unfaithful one, not his mother. In some ways, knowing this made her seem more human.

"Look, Austin," he said, "Don't worry. I'll take care of this."

"How? Olivia said—"

"They're my parents, not Olivia's."

"She said she couldn't live with herself if she exposed your mother."

That was like Olivia. "Like I said, I'll take care of this."

As soon as the call ended, Matt packed up his briefcase and headed out. He drove straight to his parents' home.

"You have your nerve, coming here like this," his mother said when he walked into her sitting room.

"We have to talk."

"We have nothing to say to one another."

"Is Dad here?"

"Your father is golfing. Now please go."

Matt suddenly felt sorry for her. Her entire world, the one she'd built so carefully, was about to fall apart. But he hardened his heart. He couldn't afford sympathy. Not when so much was at stake. "I'm not leaving until we talk about Jonathan Kendrick."

Her face stiffened with shock.

"He died last week. Did you know that?"

"J-Jon died?"

Matt saw the way her hands trembled as she clutched them in her lap, but his resolve didn't waver. He explained the circumstances of Kendrick's death as Austin had explained them. And then he told her about the will and the letter Kendrick had written to Olivia.

"Austin Crenshaw wanted to present this information to the judge on Monday, but Olivia—the same woman you have done your best to smear—told him she couldn't be a party to something like that. I, however, have no such qualms. So if you don't want the world to know about you and about the circumstances of Mark's birth, you will go to court Monday morning and drop the custody suit. Because if you continue with this vendetta against Olivia, I will expose the truth."

By now, his mother had recovered her aplomb and the sorrow he'd glimpsed earlier had disappeared. She was once again the regal ice queen ruling her kingdom. "You wouldn't dare."

"Yes, Mother, I would."

"You'd be ruining your own life. No one will vote for you for dog catcher if you go ahead with this."

"I honestly don't care."

"You're bluffing."

"I'm dead serious."

She stared at him. "You mean it."

"I do."

"I won't forgive you for this."

Matt suddenly felt exhausted. "You only have yourself to blame. I'm just the messenger. And the son you always considered second best."

"That's not true."

"Which part? The blame? Or how you've always looked at me?"

When she didn't answer, he said wearily, "All of it *is* true, but you know what? It doesn't matter anymore. Because I know exactly how you can make it all up to me…and keep your reputation intact."

She didn't interrupt as Matt told her he loved Olivia and intended to marry her, if she'd have him. "And you will not do anything to oppose our marriage or to make her unhappy. We don't have to play happy families all the time, because we won't live in Crandall Lake. Since I'll be working there, and I know Olivia wants to go back to school, I plan to buy a house in San Marcos. But no matter what, you will, at all times, be civil and you will not say one word against my wife, to anyone, ever. Do you understand? Because if you do, I promise you, you will never see Thea again, and every bit of what I found out today will be made public."

In her eyes, he could see acknowledgment that she was beaten. "So I have your word that you will call Jackson Moyer today? And instruct him to drop the custody suit?"

"Yes," she said through gritted teeth.

"And you agree to the rest of my terms?"

She nodded curtly.

Matt felt as if the weight of the world had been lifted from his shoulders as he walked out the front door. He couldn't remember ever feeling happier, and he couldn't wait to tell Olivia she no longer had to worry about anything.

Olivia was overjoyed when Austin phoned to tell her Jackson Moyer had called him to say that the Brittons were dropping the custody suit.

"You're sure?" she said.

"Yes. Apparently, after I called him, Matt convinced

your mother-in-law dropping the suit was in her best interest."

Olivia had barely hung up from the call with Austin when her phone rang again and Matt's photo popped up on the screen.

"Hi, Matt," she said, answering.

"Hey. Did Austin call you?"

"Yes."

"Good. I just wanted to be sure you knew. Listen, I'm at my office. I have a couple of things I need to wrap up, then I'm coming over. Okay?"

Olivia looked at her watch. It was three o'clock. "Okay. I'm going to take Thea to my mom's. I'll be back by four."

"See you then."

Her mother hugged her fiercely when Olivia told her the good news. "Oh, honey, I'm so happy this nightmare is over. Do you know why the Brittons backed off so suddenly?"

"Little pitchers," Olivia said, glancing at Thea, who'd gone into her mom's living room and had already pulled out the toy box her mom kept for her visits. "I'll explain everything later, okay? Right now I need to go back home." In a lower voice, she said, "Matt is coming by. We need to settle some things."

"I understand," her mother said. Then she smiled. "Give him my love."

Olivia nodded, but inside, her stomach clenched. Vivienne may have dropped the suit, but she would still hate her. In fact, she probably hated Olivia more now than she ever had. And no matter what concessions Matt might have wrung from Vivienne, she would find ways to make Olivia's life even more miserable than she had in the past. There was no way she and Matt could marry. No way they'd ever be the kind of close, loving family Olivia craved. It exhausted Olivia even to think about years and years of drama and stress.

Wouldn't Olivia be a lot better off accepting Eve and Adam's offer and moving to California? Sure, she'd miss Matt terribly, but she'd get over losing him. After all, she'd gotten over losing Mark, hadn't she? Wouldn't they all be better off if she and Thea made a fresh start far away from the Brittons?

As she drove back home, that question hounded her.

She just hoped when she finally saw Matt face-to-face today, she would know the answer and be brave enough to accept it.

Matt put on his favorite Sirius station and sang along with the radio as he drove the fifteen-mile distance between San Marcos and Crandall Lake. He felt jubilant. Although he'd always believed there would be some way to allay Olivia's fears and force his mother to accept his choice of wife, he knew now he'd always had a small particle of fear lodged down deep.

But no more.

All fear was gone. His mother no longer had any power over him or Olivia. They were free to declare their love to the world. He grinned.

Free to be together.

Free to marry.

Free to have other children, sisters and brothers for Thea.

Happiness made him laugh out loud. He couldn't wait to see her.

Olivia got back home by three forty-five. Knowing Matt would probably be right on time, she hurriedly changed her flannel shirt for a bright red sweater, ran a comb through her hair and freshened her lip gloss. Even though things might not turn out happily for them today, she still wanted to look her best.

She heard his car turn into the driveway two minutes before the hour. Her heart immediately accelerated, and she swallowed. She took several deep breaths and by the time he rang the doorbell, she felt as ready as she'd ever be.

It hurt to see the happiness on his face. It hurt to know she'd doubted him, even for an instant, because she could see the truth in his eyes. He had never lied to her, not even by omission. He *did* love her. But was his love enough? That had always been the question.

The smile on his face faded as their gazes locked. "What's wrong?"

She shook her head. "Let's go into the living room and talk."

He sat on the sofa, and she purposely sat across from him in one of the side chairs. His frown deepened. "Has something else happened that I don't know about? I would have thought you'd be jumping for joy."

In that moment, everything seemed so clear to her. But how to begin? "I'm happy about the custody suit being dropped, of course. And I'm grateful for what you did to make that happen, because I couldn't have allowed Austin to expose your mother to the world. But I've been doing a lot of thinking in the past few days. And it all boils down to this—your mother is going to resent me even more now than she ever did before. I'm sorry, Matt, but I just don't see how there will ever be any future for us."

He shook his head. "My mother won't give us any more trouble. I can promise you that."

"Why? Because you blackmailed her? Threatened her? You must have. She would never have backed down otherwise. I—I don't see how we can have any kind of future together that's built on that kind of foundation." Olivia willed herself not to cry, even though she wanted to weep at the expression on his face. She knew she was hurting him terribly, yet how could things be any different?

"This is crazy talk," he said, jumping up. "You can't really intend to allow my mother to rule the rest of your life. To ruin what we have together." Coming over to where she sat, he took her hand and pulled her to her feet. Gathering her in his arms, he held her close.

She could feel his heart beating and she closed her eyes.

"Olivia, I love you and Thea more than life itself. Life won't be worth living if I can't live it with the two of you." He stopped for a moment. "The question is, do you love me? I feel you do, but I need to hear you say it as if you mean it."

"Yes," she whispered. "I do love you, Matt. So much."

His arms tightened around her. "Then that's all that's important. Everything else can be worked out."

"But—"

Ignoring her attempt to interrupt, he said, "Listen to me. We don't have to live in Crandall Lake. We can live in San Marcos. Or, if you feel it's best to get away from my parents, I'm willing to relocate anywhere you want. As long as I'm with you, nothing else matters."

"But your life is here. Your job…"

"Is just a job. I can work anywhere."

"How? You're licensed here in Texas."

"I can take the bar in another state. Hell, I can do something different if I want to. I've invested my inheritance from my granddad Britton. Plus, my intended is a wealthy woman, isn't she?" He laughed to show her he was teasing her. Then he became earnest again. "I know how much you want a close and loving family. I've always known that. I want that, too, Olivia. But think about it. We'll have each other. We'll have Thea, and we'll have more children, won't we? We have your mother, your sister, my sister, Eve and her family. If my parents want to be a part of this, they can be. And if they don't, that's their choice, isn't it?"

Yes, she thought, it *was* their choice. Matt was right. He was right! Blinking away her tears, she looked up. Oh, God, she loved him so. "And, if necessary, you'd really consent to move somewhere else? For me?"

"I'd do anything in the world for you. I've told you that before."

Their eyes held for a long moment.

And then, smiling, he dipped his head and kissed her.

She sighed into the kiss.

They stood together for a long time. And when kissing was no longer enough, he scooped her up and carried her into her little study. This time, when they made love on the daybed, they didn't have to worry about being quiet so as not to disturb Thea. And they didn't have to hurry.

As their lovemaking reached its peak and they came together in a joyous blend of bodies and hearts, Olivia knew she had finally found the home she'd wanted for so long. "I love you, Matt." Now that she'd said it without fear and doubt, she wanted to keep saying it over and over again.

"And I love you," he murmured, wrapping his arms around her. "Let's get married right away. We can get a license on Monday and be Mr. and Mrs. Britton by the end of the week."

"I'm already Mrs. Britton," Olivia said, laughing.

He chuckled and nuzzled her neck. "Smart aleck."

"You know, when Mark and I married, it was such a hurried affair because he was leaving for Afghanistan and your mother…well, you know how your mother was. Would you think I was silly if I told you that this time, I'd like to do it right? Even if your parents don't come, I'd still like a real wedding. I want a pretty dress and I want Thea to be a flower girl and Stella and Eve to be my attendants."

"Of course, I don't think that's silly. But I also don't want to wait a long time. We're not like other couples who can move in together. There's Thea to consider."

"I know."

"So how long?"

"Two or three weeks?"

He sighed and tightened his embrace. "If we can make love again now and then again later, maybe I can survive waiting a couple of weeks."

She sighed happily. "Slave driver."

"Quit wasting time talking."

* * * * *

Don't miss the other books in Patricia Kay's
THE CRANDALL LAKE CHRONICLES,
THE GIRL HE LEFT BEHIND
&
OH, BABY!

Available now wherever Harlequin Special Edition books and ebooks are sold!

Norma Dubrovnik's Haluski (Noodles & Cabbage)

1 small head of cabbage
1 16-ounce package of flat noodles
2 medium-sized white or yellow onions (or more, if you like)
Olive oil (original recipe called for butter)
Salt and pepper

Peel and slice onions into thin slices. Slice cabbage into thin slices. Sauté onions and cabbage on low-to-medium heat in olive oil in large skillet until tender. This process can be speeded up by lowering heat even more and covering skillet. Be sure to turn often so vegetables don't burn. While vegetables are cooking, prepare noodles according to package directions. Drain well. Add cooked noodles to the frying pan with the cooked vegetables and toss well. Adding several tablespoons of butter to taste is optional. Add salt and pepper to taste. Can be served as a main dish or as a side dish.

Note from Patricia Kay: This recipe is one my mother made all the time when my sisters and I were growing up. It's still a family favorite.

Norma Dubrovnik's Kolache

Yield = 6 rolls
Start early, dough has to rise twice.

Dough:
6 cups sifted flour
½ cup sugar
1 ½ sticks margarine or butter (softened)
2 cups milk (let stand at room temperature)
1 package dry yeast
2 eggs (at room temperature)
1 ½ teaspoons vanilla

Mix first two ingredients together. Dissolve yeast in ½ cup warm water with 1 teaspoon sugar (let stand 10 minutes). In a separate bowl, mix eggs with lukewarm milk, add vanilla. Add yeast and egg mixture to flour mixture.

Knead dough until easy to work with.

Let dough rise for about 2 hours until double the size you started with.

Nut Filling:
1 pound pecans or walnuts = 3 rolls of kolache

Grind the nuts in a food grinder or process in food processor. Add ⅓ cup of warm milk and ⅔ cup sugar for each 2 cups of nuts. Mix well. Then beat one egg white until stiff, add a teaspoon of sugar, mix all ingredients together.

Apricot Filling:
Use homemade or store-bought prepared apricot cake or pastry filling.

To Bake:
Grease cookie sheets. Divide dough into balls. Roll into an oval shape on floured board. Spread filling evenly over the dough (not too thick). Roll lengthwise, like a jelly roll. Cover filled rolls with a clean dish towel and let rise for about 1 hour.

Before baking, brush tops and sides of rolls with milk. Bake at 350 degrees for 35–40 minutes. Cool thoroughly before slicing. Serve with butter. Makes a wonderful, special breakfast treat or dessert anytime. Can be frozen.

Note from Patricia Kay: My husband and I made this recipe only once before he passed away. We experimented, because the original recipe, told to me by my mother before she passed away, was for twelve rolls at a time. (She always gave some to family members). Some of the ingredient amounts had to be adjusted, but our experiment turned out to be delicious. I know my mom will be smiling down at anyone who tries her recipe. Enjoy!

*Single mom Andrea Montgomery only agreed
to look in on injured sheriff Marshall Bailey as
a favor to his sister, but when these lonely hearts
are snowed in together, there's no telling
what Christmas wishes might come true.*

*Turn the page for a sneak peek of
SNOWFALL ON HAVEN POINT*
by New York Times *bestselling author
RaeAnne Thayne,
available October 2016
wherever Harlequin books and ebooks are sold!*

CHAPTER ONE

SHE REALLY NEEDED to learn how to say no once in a while.

Andrea Montgomery stood on the doorstep of the small, charming stone house just down the street from hers on Riverbend Road, her arms loaded with a tray of food that was cooling by the minute in the icy December wind blowing off the Hell's Fury River.

Her hands on the tray felt clammy and the flock of butterflies that seemed to have taken up permanent residence in her stomach jumped around maniacally. She didn't want to be here. Marshall Bailey, the man on the other side of that door, made her nervous under the best of circumstances.

This moment definitely did not fall into that category.

How could she turn down any request from Wynona Bailey, though? She owed Wynona whatever she wanted. The woman had taken a bullet for her, after all. If Wyn wanted her to march up and down the main drag in Haven Point wearing a tutu and combat boots, she would rush right out and try to find the perfect ensemble.

She would almost prefer that to Wyn's actual request but her friend had sounded desperate when she called earlier that day from Boise, where she was in graduate school to become a social worker.

"It's only for a week or so, until I can wrap things

up here with my practicum and Mom and Uncle Mike make it back from their honeymoon," Wyn had said.

"It's not a problem at all," she had assured her. Apparently she was better at telling fibs than she thought because Wynona didn't even question her.

"Trust my brother to break his leg the one week that his mother and both of his sisters are completely unavailable to help him. I think he did it on purpose."

"Didn't you tell me he was struck by a hit-and-run driver?"

"Yes, but the timing couldn't be worse, with Katrina out of the country and Mom and Uncle Mike on their cruise until the end of the week. Marshall assures me he doesn't need help, but the man has a compound fracture, for crying out loud. He's not supposed to be weight-bearing at all. I would feel better the first few days he's home from the hospital if I knew that someone who lived close by could keep an eye on him."

Andie didn't want to be that someone. But how could she say no to Wynona?

It was a good thing her friend had been a police officer until recently. If Wynona had wanted a partner in crime, *Thelma & Louise* style, Andie wasn't sure she could have said no.

"Aren't you going to ring the doorbell, Mama?" Chloe asked, eyes apprehensive and her voice wavering a little. Her daughter was picking up her own nerves, Andie knew, with that weird radar kids had, but she had also become much more timid and anxious since the terrifying incident that summer when Wyn and Cade Emmett had rescued them all.

"I can do it," her four-year-old son, Will, offered. "My feet are *freezing* out here."

Her heart filled with love for both of her funny,

sweet, wonderful children. Will was the spitting image of Jason while Chloe had his mouth and his eyes.

This would be their third Christmas without him and she had to hope she could make it much better than the previous two.

She repositioned the tray and forced herself to focus on the matter at hand. "Sorry, I was thinking of something else."

She couldn't very well tell her children that she hadn't knocked yet because she was too busy thinking about how much she didn't want to be here.

"I told you that Sheriff Bailey has a broken leg and can't get around very well. He probably can't make it to the door easily and I don't want to make him get up. He should be expecting us. Wynona said she was calling him."

She transferred the tray to one arm just long enough to knock a couple of times loudly and twist the doorknob, which gave way easily. The door was blessedly unlocked.

"Sheriff Bailey? Hello? It's Andrea Montgomery."

"And Will and Chloe Montgomery," her son called helpfully, and Andie had to smile, despite the nerves jangling through her.

An instant later, she heard a crash, a thud and a muffled groan.

"Sheriff Bailey?"

"Not really…a good time."

She couldn't miss the pain in the voice of Wynona's older brother. It made her realize how ridiculous she was being. The man had been through a terrible ordeal in the last twenty-four hours and all she could think about was how much he intimidated her.

Nice, Andie. Feeling small and ashamed, she set the

tray down on the nearest flat surface, a small table in the foyer still decorated in Wyn's quirky, fun style even though her brother had been living in the home since late August.

"Kids, wait right here for a moment," she said.

Chloe immediately planted herself on the floor by the door, her features taking on the fearful look she had worn too frequently since Rob Warren burst back into their lives so violently. Will, on the other hand, looked bored already. How had her children's roles reversed so abruptly? Chloe used to be the brave one, charging enthusiastically past any challenge, while Will had been the more tentative child.

"Do you need help?" Chloe asked tentatively.

"No. Stay here. I'll be right back."

She was sure the sound had come from the room where Wyn had spent most of her time when she lived here, a space that served as den, family room and TV viewing room in one. Her gaze immediately went to Marshall Bailey, trying to heft himself back up to the sofa from the floor.

"Oh no!" she exclaimed. "What happened?"

"What do you think happened?" he growled. "You knocked on the door, so I tried to get up to answer and the damn crutches slipped out from under me."

"I'm so sorry. I only knocked to give you a little warning before we barged in. I didn't mean for you to get up."

He glowered. "Then you shouldn't have come over and knocked on the door."

She hated any conversation that came across as a confrontation. They always made her want to hide away in her room like she was a teenager again in her grandfather's house. It was completely immature of her, she knew. Grown-ups couldn't always walk away.

"Wyn asked me to check on you. Didn't she tell you?"

"I haven't talked to her since yesterday. My phone ran out of juice and I haven't had a chance to charge it."

By now, the county sheriff had pulled himself back onto the sofa and was trying to position pillows for his leg that sported a black orthopedic boot from his toes to just below his knee. His features contorted as he tried to reach the pillows but he quickly smoothed them out again. The man was obviously in pain and doing his best to conceal it.

She couldn't leave him to suffer, no matter how nervous his gruff demeanor made her.

She hurried forward and pulled the second pillow into place. "Is that how you wanted it?" she asked.

"For now."

She had a sudden memory of seeing the sheriff the night Rob Warren had broken into her home, assaulted her, held her at gunpoint and ended up in a shoot-out with the Haven Point police chief, Cade Emmett. He had burst into her home after the situation had been largely defused, to find Cade on the ground trying to revive a bleeding Wynona.

The stark fear on Marshall's face had haunted her, knowing that she might have unwittingly contributed to him losing another sibling after he had already lost his father and a younger brother in the line of duty.

Now Marshall's features were a shade or two paler and his eyes had the glassy, distant look of someone in a great deal of pain.

"How long have you been out of the hospital?"

He shrugged. "A couple hours. Give or take."

"And you're here by yourself?" she exclaimed. "I thought you were supposed to be home earlier this morning and someone was going to stay with you for the first few hours. Wynona told me that was the plan."

"One of my deputies drove me home from the hospital but I told him Chief Emmett would probably keep an eye on me."

The police chief lived across the street from Andie and just down the street from Marshall, which boded well for crime prevention in the neighborhood. Having the sheriff *and* the police chief on the same street should be any sane burglar's worst nightmare—especially *this* particular sheriff and police chief.

"And has he been by?"

"Uh, no. I didn't ask him to." Marshall's eyes looked unnaturally blue in his pain-tight features. "Did my sister send you to babysit me?"

"Babysit, no. She only asked me to periodically check on you. I also brought dinner for the next few nights."

"Also unnecessary. If I get hungry, I'll call Serrano's for a pizza later."

She gave him a bland look. "Would a pizza delivery driver know to come pick you up off the floor?"

"You didn't pick me up," he muttered. "You just moved a few pillows around."

He must find this completely intolerable, being dependent on others for the smallest thing. In her limited experience, most men made difficult patients. Tough, take-charge guys like Marshall Bailey probably hated every minute of it.

Sympathy and compassion had begun to replace some of her nervousness. She would probably never truly like the man—he was so big, so masculine, a cop through and through—but she could certainly empathize with what he was going through. For now, he was a victim and she certainly knew what that felt like.

"I brought dinner, so you might as well eat it," she said. "You can order pizza tomorrow if you want. It's not much, just beef stew and homemade rolls, with caramel apple pie for dessert."

"Not much?" he said, eyebrow raised. A low rumble sounded in the room just then and it took her a moment to realize it was coming from his stomach.

"You don't have to eat it, but if you'd like some, I can bring it in here."

He opened his mouth but before he could answer, she heard a voice from the doorway.

"What happened to you?" Will asked, gazing at Marshall's assorted scrapes, bruises and bandages with wide-eyed fascination.

"Will, I thought I told you to wait for me by the door."

"I know, but you were taking *forever*." He walked into the room a little farther, not at all intimidated by the battered, dangerous-looking man it contained. "Hi. My name is Will. What's yours?"

The sheriff gazed at her son. If anything, his features became even more remote, but he might have simply been in pain.

"This is Sheriff Bailey," Andie said, when Marshall didn't answer for a beat too long. "He's Wynona's brother."

Will beamed at him as if Marshall was his new best friend. "Wynona is nice and she has a nice dog whose name is Young Pete, only Wynona said he's not young anymore."

"Yeah, I know Young Pete," Marshall said after another pause. "He's been in our family for a long time. He was our dad's dog first."

Andie gave him a careful look. From Wyn, she knew their father had been shot in the line of duty several years earlier and had suffered a severe brain injury that left him physically and cognitively impaired. John Bailey had died the previous winter from pneumonia, after spending his last years at a Shelter Springs care center.

Though she had never met the man, her heart ached to think of all the Baileys had suffered.

"Why is his name Young Pete?" Will asked. "I think that's silly. He should be just Pete."

"Couldn't agree more, but you'll have to take that up with my sister."

Will accepted that with equanimity. He took another step closer and scrutinized the sheriff. "How did you get so hurt? Were you in a fight with some bad guys? Did you shoot them? A bad guy came to our house once and Chief Emmett shot him."

Andie stepped in quickly. She was never sure how much Will understood about what happened that summer. "Will, I need your help fixing a tray with dinner for the sheriff."

"I want to hear about the bad guys, though."

"There were no bad guys. I was hit by a car," Marshall said abruptly.

"You're big! Don't you know you're supposed to look both ways and hold someone's hand?"

Marshall Bailey's expression barely twitched. "I guess nobody happened to be around at the time."

Torn between amusement and mortification, Andie grabbed her son's hand. "Come on, Will," she said, her tone insistent. "I need your help."

Her put-upon son sighed. "Okay."

He let her hold his hand as they went back to the entry, where Chloe still sat on the floor, watching the hallway with anxious eyes.

"I told Will not to go in when you told us to wait here but he wouldn't listen to me," Chloe said fretfully.

"You should see the police guy," Will said with relish. "He has blood on him and everything."

Andie hadn't seen any blood but maybe Will was more observant than she. Or maybe he had just become good at trying to get a rise out of his sister.

"Ew. Gross," Chloe exclaimed, looking at the doorway with an expression that contained equal parts revulsion and fascination.

"He is Wyn's brother and knows Young Pete, too," Will informed her.

Easily distracted, as most six-year-old girls could be, Chloe sighed. "I miss Young Pete. I wonder if he and Sadie will be friends?"

"Why wouldn't they be?" Will asked.

"Okay, kids, we can talk about Sadie and Young Pete another time. Right now, we need to get dinner for Wynona's brother."

"I need to use the bathroom," Will informed her. He had that urgent look he sometimes wore when he had pushed things past the limit.

"There's a bathroom just down the hall, second door down. See?"

"Okay."

He raced for it—she hoped in time.

"We'll be in the kitchen," she told him, then carried the food to the bright and spacious room with its stainless appliances and white cabinets.

"See if you can find a small plate for the pie while I dish up the stew," she instructed Chloe.

"Okay," her daughter said.

The nervous note in her voice broke Andie's heart, especially when she thought of the bold child who used to run out to confront the world.

"Do I have to carry it out there?" Chloe asked.

"Not if you don't want to, honey. You can wait right here in the kitchen or in the entryway, if you want."

While Chloe perched on one of the kitchen stools and watched, Andie prepared a tray for him, trying to make it as tempting as possible. She had a feeling his appetite wouldn't be back to normal for a few days because of the pain and the aftereffects of anesthesia but at least the fault wouldn't lie in her presentation.

It didn't take long, but it still gave her time to make note of the few changes in the kitchen. In the few months Wynona had been gone, Marshall Bailey had left his mark. The kitchen was clean but not sparkling, and where Wyn had kept a cheery bowl of fruit on the counter, a pair of handcuffs and a stack of mail cluttered the space. Young Pete's food and water bowls were presumably in Boise with Young Pete.

As she looked at the space on the floor where they usually rested, she suddenly remembered dogs weren't the only creatures who needed beverages.

"I forgot to fill Sheriff Bailey's water bottle," she said to Chloe. "Could you do that for me?"

Chloe hopped down from her stool and picked up the water bottle. With her bottom lip pressed firmly between her teeth, she filled the water bottle with ice and water from the refrigerator before screwing the lid back on and held it out for Andie.

"Thanks, honey. Oh, the tray's pretty full and I don't have a free hand. I guess I'll have to make another trip for it."

As she had hoped, Chloe glanced at the tray and then at the doorway with trepidation on her features that eventually shifted to resolve.

"I guess I can maybe carry it for you," she whispered.

Andie smiled and rubbed a hand over her hair, heart bursting with pride at this brave little girl. "Thank you, Chloe. You're always such a big help to me."

Chloe mustered a smile, though it didn't stick. "You'll be right there?"

"The whole time. Where do you suppose that brother of yours is?"

She suspected the answer, even before she and Chloe walked back to the den and she heard Will chattering.

"And I want a new Lego set and a sled and some real walkie-talkies like my friend Ty has. He has his own pony and I want one of those, too, only my mama says I can't have one because we don't have a place for him to run. Ty lives on a ranch and we only have a little backyard and we don't have a barn or any hay for him to eat. That's what horses eat—did you know that?"

Rats. Had she actually been stupid enough to fall for that "I have to go to the bathroom" gag? She should have known better. Will had probably raced right back in here the moment her back was turned.

"I did know that. And oats and barley, too," Sheriff Bailey said. His voice, several octaves below Will's, rippled down her spine. Did he sound annoyed? She couldn't tell. Mostly, his voice sounded remote.

"We have oatmeal at our house and my mom puts barley in soup sometimes, so why couldn't we have a pony?"

She should probably rescue the man. He just had one leg broken by a hit-and-run driver. He didn't need the other one talked off by an almost-five-year-old. She moved into the room just in time to catch the tail end of the discussion.

"A pony is a pretty big responsibility," Marshall said.

"So is a dog and a cat and we have one of each, a dog named Sadie and a cat named Mrs. Finnegan," Will pointed out.

"But a pony is a lot more work than a dog *or* a cat. Anyway, how would one fit on Santa's sleigh?"

Judging by his peal of laughter, Will apparently thought that was hilarious.

"He couldn't! You're silly."

She had to wonder if anyone had ever called the serious sheriff *silly* before. She winced and carried the tray inside the room, judging it was past time to step in.

"Here you go. Dinner. Again, don't get your hopes up. I'm an adequate cook but that's about it."

She set the food down on the end table next to the sofa and found a folded wooden TV tray she didn't remember from her frequent visits to the house when Wynona lived here. She set up the TV tray and transferred the food to it, then gestured for Chloe to bring the water bottle. Her daughter hurried over without meeting his gaze, set the bottle on the tray, then rushed back to the safety of the kitchen as soon as she could.

Marshall looked at the tray, then at her, leaving her feeling as if *she* were the silly one.

"Thanks. It looks good. I appreciate your kindness," he said stiffly, as if the words were dragged out of him.

He had to know any kindness on her part was out of obligation toward Wynona. The thought made her feel rather guilty. He was her neighbor and she should be more enthusiastic about helping him, whether he made her nervous or not.

"Where is your cell phone?" she asked. "You need some way to contact the outside world."

"Why?"

She frowned. "Because people are concerned about you! You just got out of the hospital a few hours ago. You need pain medicine at regular intervals and you're probably supposed to have ice on that leg or something."

"I'm fine, as long as I can get to the bathroom and the kitchen and I have the remote close at hand."

Such a typical man. She huffed out a breath. "At least think of the people who care about you. Wyn is out of her head with worry, especially since your mother and Katrina aren't in town."

"Why do you think I didn't charge my phone?" he muttered.

She crossed her arms across her chest. She didn't like confrontation or big, dangerous men any more than her daughter did, but Wynona had asked her to watch out for him and she took the charge seriously.

"You're being obstinate. What if you trip over your crutches and hit your head, only this time somebody isn't at the door to make sure you can get up again?"

"That's not going to happen."

"You don't know that. Where is your phone, Sheriff?"

He glowered at her but seemed to accept the inevitable. "Fine," he said with a sigh. "It should be in the pocket of my jacket, which is in the bag they sent home with me from the hospital. I think my deputy said he left it in the bedroom. First door on the left."

The deputy should have made sure his boss had some way to contact the outside world, but she had a feeling it was probably a big enough chore getting Sheriff Bailey home from the hospital without him trying to drive himself and she decided to give the poor guy some slack.

"I'm going to assume the charger is in there, too."

"Yeah. By the bed."

She walked down the hall to the room that had once been Wyn's bedroom. The bedroom still held traces of Wynona in the solid Mission furniture set but Sheriff Bailey had stamped his own personality on it in the last three months. A Stetson hung on one of the bedposts, and instead of mounds of pillows and the beautiful log cabin quilt Wyn's aunts had made her, a no-frills but soft-looking navy duvet covered the bed, made neatly as he had probably left it the morning before. A pile of books waited on the bedside table and a pair of battered cowboy boots stood toe-out next to the closet.

The room smelled masculine and entirely too sexy for her peace of mind, of sage-covered mountains with an undertone of leather and spice.

Except for that brief moment when she had helped him back to the sofa, she had never been close enough to Marshall to see if that scent clung to his skin. The idea made her shiver a little before she managed to rein in the wholly inappropriate reaction.

She found the plastic hospital bag on the wide armchair near the windows, overlooking the snow-covered pines along the river. Feeling strangely guilty at invading the man's privacy, she opened it. At the top of the pile that appeared to contain mostly clothing, she found another large clear bag with a pair of ripped jeans inside covered in a dried dark substance she realized was blood.

Marshall Bailey's blood.

The stark reminder of his close call sent a tremor through her. He could have been killed if that hit-and-run driver had struck him at a slightly higher rate of speed. The Baileys likely wouldn't have recovered, especially since Wyn's twin brother, Wyatt, had been struck and killed by an out-of-control vehicle while helping a stranded motorist during a winter storm.

The jeans weren't ruined beyond repair. Maybe she could spray stain remover on them and try to mend the rips and tears.

Further searching through the bag finally unearthed the telephone. She found the charger next to the bed and carried the phone, charger and bag containing the Levi's back to the sheriff.

While she was gone from the room, he had pulled the tray close and was working on the dinner roll in a desultory way.

She plugged the charger into the same outlet as the lamp next to the sofa and inserted the other end into his phone. "Here you are. I'll let you turn it on. Now you'll have no excuse not to talk to your family when they call."

"Thanks. I guess."

Andie held out the bag containing the jeans. "Do you mind if I take these? I'd like to see if I can get the stains out and do a little repair work."

"It's not worth the effort. I don't even know why they sent them home. The paramedics had to cut them away to get to my leg."

"You never know. I might be able to fix them."

He shrugged, his eyes wearing that distant look again. He was in pain, she realized, and trying very hard not to show it.

"If you power on your phone and unlock it, I can put my cell number in there so you can reach me in an emergency."

"I won't—" he started to say but the sentence ended with a sigh as he reached for the phone.

As soon as he turned it on, the phone gave a cacophony of beeps, alerting him to missed texts and messages, but he paid them no attention.

"What's your number?"

She gave it to him and in turn entered his into her own phone.

"Please don't be stubborn. If you need help, call me. I'm just a few houses away and can be here in under two minutes—and that's even if I have to take time to put on boots and a winter coat."

He likely wouldn't call and both of them knew it.

"Are we almost done?" Will asked from the doorway, clearly tired of having only his sister to talk to in the other room.

"In a moment," she said, then turned back to Marshall. "Do you know Herm and Louise Jacobs, next door?"

Oddly, he gaped at her for a long, drawn-out moment. "Why do you ask?" His voice was tight with suspicion.

"If I'm not around and you need help for some reason, they or their grandson Christopher can be here even faster. I'll put their number in your phone, too, just in case."

"I doubt I'll need it, but...thanks."

"Christopher has a skateboard, a big one," Will offered gleefully. "He rides it without even a helmet!"

Her son had a bad case of hero worship when it came to the Jacobses' troubled grandson, who had come to live with Herm and Louise shortly after Andie and her children arrived in Haven Point. It worried her a little to see how fascinated Will was with the clearly rebellious teenager, but so far Christopher had been patient and even kind to her son.

"That's not very safe, is it?" the sheriff said gruffly. "You should always wear a helmet when you're riding a bike or skateboard to protect your head."

"I don't even *have* a skateboard," Will said.

"If you get one," Marshall answered. This time she couldn't miss the clear strain in his voice. The man was at the end of his endurance and probably wanted nothing more than to be alone with his pain.

"We really do need to leave," Andie said quickly. "Is there anything else I can do to help you before we leave?"

He shook his head, then winced a little as if the motion hurt. "You've done more than enough already."

"Try to get some rest, if you can. I'll check in with you tomorrow and also bring something for your lunch."

He didn't exactly look overjoyed at the prospect. "I don't suppose I can say anything to persuade you otherwise, can I?"

"You're a wise man, Sheriff Bailey."

Will giggled. "Where's your gold and Frankenstein?"

Marshall blinked, obviously as baffled as she was, which only made Will giggle more.

"Like in the Baby Jesus story, you know. The wise men brought the gold, Frankenstein and mirth."

She did her best to hide a smile. This year Will had become fascinated with the small carved Nativity set she bought at a thrift store the first year she moved out of her grandfather's cheerless house.

"Oh. Frankincense and myrrh. They were perfumes and oils, I think. When I said Sheriff Bailey was a wise man, I just meant he was smart."

She was a little biased, yes, but she couldn't believe

even the most hardened of hearts wouldn't find her son adorable. The sheriff only studied them both with that dour expression.

He was in pain, she reminded herself. If she were in his position, she wouldn't find a four-year-old's chatter amusing, either.

"We'll see you tomorrow," she said again. "Call me, even if it's the middle of the night."

"I will," he said, which she knew was a blatant fib. He would never call her.

She had done all she could, short of moving into his house—kids, pets and all.

She gathered the children part of that equation and ushered them out of the house. Darkness came early this close to the winter solstice but the Jacobs family's Christmas lights next door gleamed through the snow.

In the short time she'd been inside his house, Andie had forgotten most of her nervousness around Marshall. Perhaps it was his injury that made him feel a little less threatening to her—though she had a feeling that even if he'd suffered *two* broken legs in that accident, the sheriff of Lake Haven County would never be anything less than dangerous.

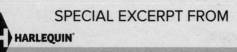
"Why do you care, Caleb?"

He was silent for so long she wasn't sure he was going to answer. And since he wasn't, she pushed away from the brick. "I need to get back to Tyler."

"I've always cared."

His words washed over her. Instead of feeling like a balmy wave, though, it felt like being rolled against abrasive sand. "Right." She stepped around him.

"Dammit." His hand shot out and he grabbed her arm. She tried to shaking him off. "Let go."

"You asked and I'm telling you. So now you're going to walk away?" He let her go. "I swear, you're as stubborn as your mother."

She flinched.

He swore again. Thrust his fingers through his dark hair. "I didn't mean that."

Why not? She adored her son. Didn't regret his existence for one single second. In that, she was very different from her mother. But that didn't mean she wasn't Georgette Rasmussen's daughter with all the rest that that implied.

"I have to go." She tried stepping around his big body again.

"I'm sorry that I hurt you. I was always sorry, Kelly. Always."

She looked up at him. "But you did it anyway."

"And you're going to hate me forever because of it? It was nearly ten years ago!"

When he'd dumped her for another girl.

And only six years when she'd impetuously, angrily put her mouth on his and set in motion a situation she still couldn't change.

Which was worse?

His actions or hers?

Her eyes suddenly burned. Because she was pretty sure keeping the existence of his own son from him outweighed him falling in love with someone far better suited to him than simple little Kelly Rasmussen.

He made a rough sound of impatience. "If you're gonna hate me anyway—"

She barely had a chance to frown before his mouth hit hers.

Don't miss
A CHILD UNDER HIS TREE by Allison Leigh,
available November 2016 wherever
Harlequin® Special Edition books and ebooks are sold.

www.Harlequin.com

$7.99 U.S./$9.99 CAN.

EXCLUSIVE
Limited Time Offer

$1.⁰⁰ OFF

New York Times bestselling author

RaeAnne Thayne

There's no place like Haven Point for the holidays, where the snow conspires to bring two wary hearts together for a Christmas to remember.

SNOWFALL ON HAVEN POINT

Available September 27, 2016.
Pick up your copy today!

HQN™

$1.⁰⁰ OFF the purchase price of SNOWFALL ON HAVEN POINT by RaeAnne Thayne.

Offer valid from September 27, 2016, to October 31, 2016.
Redeemable at participating retail outlets. Not redeemable at Barnes & Noble.
Limit one coupon per purchase. Valid in the U.S.A. and Canada only.

52613933

5 65373 00076 2 (8100)0 12185

® and ™ are trademarks owned and used by the trademark owner and/or its licensee.

PHCOUPRAT1016

JUST CAN'T GET ENOUGH?

Join our social communities
and talk to us online.

You will have access to the latest
news on upcoming titles and special
promotions, but most importantly,
you can talk to other fans about your
favorite Harlequin reads.

Harlequin.com/Community

Facebook.com/HarlequinBooks

Twitter.com/HarlequinBooks

Pinterest.com/HarlequinBooks